REMY

BAYOU BROTHERHOOD PROTECTORS
BOOK ONE

ELLE JAMES

TWISTED PAGE INC

REMY

BAYOU BROTHERHOOD PROTECTORS
BOOK #1

New York Times & USA Today
Bestselling Author

ELLE JAMES

Copyright © 2023 by Elle James

All rights reserved.

No part of this book may be reproduced in any form or by any electronic or mechanical means, including information storage and retrieval systems, without written permission from the author, except for the use of brief quotations in a book review.

© 2023 Twisted Page Inc. All rights reserved.

ISBN EBOOK: 978-1-62695-516-5

ISBN PRINT: 978-1-62695-517-2

*To Delilah, Courtney, Jenn, and Bev who are always up
for a little brainstorming. Love you all!*
Elle James

AUTHOR'S NOTE

Enjoy other protector books by Elle James

Bayou Brotherhood Protectors
Remy (#1)
Gerard (#2)
Lucas (#3)
Beau (#4)
Rafael (#5)
Valentin (#6)
Landry (#7)
Simon (#8)
Maurice (#9)
Jacques (#10)

Visit ellejames.com for more titles and release dates
Join her newsletter at
https://ellejames.com/contact/

CHAPTER 1

With the sun dipping over the treetops and dusk settling beneath the boughs of the cypress trees, Deputy Shelby Taylor checked her watch. It would be dark before long. She should be turning around and heading back to the town of Bayou Mambaloa.

Named after the bayou on the edge of which it perched, the town was Shelby's home, where she'd been born and raised. But for a seven-year break, she'd lived in that small town all of her life.

So many young people left Bayou Mambaloa as soon as they turned eighteen. Many went to college or left for employment in New Orleans, Baton Rouge, Houston or some other city. Good-paying jobs were scarce in Bayou Mambaloa unless you were a fishing guide or the owner of a bed and breakfast. The primary industries keeping the town alive were tourism and fishing.

Thankfully, between the two of them, there was enough work for the small town to thrive for at least nine months of the year. The three months of cooler weather gave the residents time to regroup, restock, paint and get ready for the busy part of the year.

As small as Bayou Mambaloa was, it had an inordinate amount of crime per capita. Thus necessitating a sheriff's department and sheriff's deputies, who worked the 911 dispatch calls, responding to everything from rogue alligators in residential pools to drug smuggling.

Shelby sighed. Having grown up on the bayou, she knew her way around on land and in the water.

Her father had always wanted a boy. When all her mother had produced was Shelby and her sister, he hadn't let that slow him down. A fishing guide, her father had taken her out fishing nearly three-hundred-and-sixty-five days of the year, allowing her to steer whatever watercraft he had at the time—pirogues, canoes, bass boats, Jon boats and even an airboat.

Whenever a call came needing someone to get out on the bayou, her name was first on the list. She had to admit that she preferred patrolling in a boat versus in one of the SUVs in the department's fleet. Still, there were so many tributaries, islands, twists and turns in the bayou that if smugglers hid there, they'd be hard to find, even for Shelby.

She'd been on the water since seven o'clock that

morning after an anonymous caller had reported seeing two men on an airboat offloading several wooden crates onto an island in the bayou.

The report came on the heels of a heads-up from a Narcotics Detective with the Louisiana State Police's Criminal Investigations Division.

An informant had said that a drug cartel had set up shop in or near Bayou Mambaloa. The parish Sheriff's Department was to report anything they might find that was suspicious or indicative of drug running in their area.

Because the tip had been anonymous, Sheriff Bergeron had sent Shelby out to investigate and report her findings. She was not to engage, just mark the spot with her GPS and get that information back as soon as possible.

The caller had given a general location, which could have included any number of islands.

Shelby had circled at least ten islands during the day, walked the length of half of them and found nothing.

The only time she'd returned to Marcelle's Marina had been to fill the boat's gas tank and grab a sandwich and more water. At that time, she'd checked in with Sheriff Bergeron. He hadn't had any more calls and hadn't heard from CID. With nothing pressing going on elsewhere in the parish, he'd had Shelby continue her search.

Normally, any chance to get out of the patrol car

and on the water was heaven for Shelby. Not that day. Oppressive, late summer heat bore down on her all day. With humidity at ninety-seven percent, she'd started sweating at eight in the morning, consumed a gallon of water and was completely drenched.

She wished it would go ahead and rain to wash away the stench of her perspiration. Maybe, in the process, the rain would lower the temperature to less than hell's fiery inferno.

She passed a weathered fishing shack and sighed as she read the fading sign painted in blue letters— The Later Gator Fishing Hut. She released the throttle and let the skiff float slowly by.

A rush of memories flooded through her, bringing a sad smile to her lips. Less than a month ago, she'd spent a stormy night in that shack with a man she'd harbored a school-girl crush on for over twenty years.

She'd insisted it would only be a one-night stand they'd both walk away from with no regrets. She didn't regret that night or making love to the man. It had been an amazing night, and the sex had been better than she'd ever dreamed it could be.

However, despite her reassurances to him, she'd come away with one regret.

It had only been one night.

She wanted more.

But that wasn't to be. He'd gone on to the job waiting for him in Montana, never looking back.

He'd left Bayou Mambaloa twenty years ago. His short visit hadn't been enough to bring him back for good.

She hadn't been enough to make him want to stay.

Shelby gave the motor a surge of gas, sending the skiff away from the hut, but her memories followed. Focusing on the waterway ahead, she tried to banish the man and the memories from her thoughts.

By the time she headed back to Marcelle's Marina, the heat had taken its toll. She was tired, cranky and not at her best.

Shelby almost missed the airboat parked in an inlet half-hidden among the drooping boughs of a cypress tree. If movement out of the corner of her eye hadn't caught her attention, she would have driven her boat past without noting the coordinates.

When she turned, she spotted two men climbing aboard an airboat filled with wooden crates.

At the same moment, the taller one of the two men spotted her, grabbed the other man's arm and pointed in her direction.

"Fuck," Shelby muttered and fumbled to capture the coordinates with her cell phone, knowing she wasn't supposed to engage. If these were truly drug smugglers, they would be heavily armed.

The tall man pulled a handgun out of his waistband, aimed at Shelby and fired.

As soon as the gun came out, Shelby ducked.

Though it missed her, the bullet hit the side of her boat.

She dropped her cell phone, hit the throttle and sent the skiff powering through the bayou as fast as the outboard motor would take her.

Another shot rang out over the sound of the engine. The bullet glanced off the top of the motor, cracking the casing, but the engine roared on.

Her heart pounding like a snare drum at a rock concert, Shelby sped through the water, spun around fields of tall marsh grass, hunkering low while hoping she would disappear from their sight long enough to lose herself in the bayou.

For a moment, she dared believe she'd succeeded as she skimmed past a long stretch of marsh grass. She raised her head to peer over the vegetation, looking back in the direction of the two men.

To her immediate right, bright headlights dispelled the dusky darkness as the airboat cleaved a path through the marsh grass, blasting toward her.

Her skiff, with its outboard motor, was no match for the other craft. She had to steer around marsh grass or risk getting her propeller tangled, which meant zig-zagging through the bayou to avoid vegetation.

Not the airboat. Instead of going around, it cut through the field of grass, barreling straight for Shelby in her skiff.

She spun the bow to the left, but not soon enough to avoid the collision.

The larger airboat rammed into the front of the small skiff. The force of the blow launched the skiff into the air.

Shelby was thrown into the water and sank into darkness to the silty floor of the bayou.

As she scrambled to get her bearings and struggled to swim to the surface, the skiff came down hard over her. If not for the water's surface breaking the boat's fall, it would have crushed her and broken her neck. Instead, the hard metal smacked her hard, sending her back down into the silt. Her lungs burned, and her vision blurred.

Her mind numbing, she had only one thought.

Air.

The black water of the bayou dragged at her clothing. The silt at her feet sucked her deeper.

Her head spun, and pain throbbed through her skull. She used every last ounce of strength and consciousness and pushed her booted feet into the silt, sending herself upward. As she surfaced, her head hit something hard, sending her back beneath the water before she could fill her lungs.

Shelby surfaced a second time, her cheek scraping the side of something as she breached the surface and sucked in a deep breath.

She blinked. Were her eyes even open? The darkness was so complete she wondered for a second if the blow making her head throb and her thoughts blur had blinded her. Or was this how it felt to be dead?

She raised her hand to touch the object that had scraped her cheek. Metal. In the back of her mind, she knew she was still in the boat, but it was upside-down. The metal in front of her was the bench she'd been seated on moments before. She wrapped her fingers around the bench to keep her head above water in the air pocket between the bottom of the boat and the bayou's surface.

A whirring sound moved away and then returned, growing louder the closer it came to the inverted skiff. It slowed as it approached. Then metal clanked against metal, and the skiff lurched, the bow dipping lower into the water.

Still holding onto the bench, Shelby's murky brain registered danger. She held on tightly to the bench as the skiff was pushed through the water.

The whir outside increased along with the sound of metal scraping on metal. The front end of the skiff dipped low in the water, dipping the hull lower. Soon, Shelby's head touched the bottom of the boat, and her nose barely cleared the surface.

Whatever was moving the skiff was forcing it deeper.

Shelby had to get out from beneath the boat or drown. Tipping her head back, she breathed in a last breath, released the bench and grabbed for the side of the skiff. She pulled herself toward the edge, ducked beneath it and swam as hard as she could, her efforts jerky, her clothes weighing her down. She couldn't see her hands in front of her, and her lungs screamed for air.

When she thought she couldn't go another inch further, her hands bumped into stalks. She wrapped her fingers around them and pulled herself between them, snaking her way into a forest of reeds. Once her feet bumped against them, she lifted her head above the water and sucked in air. For a moment, the darkness wasn't as dark; the thickening dusk and the glow of headlights gave her just enough light to make out the dark strands of marsh grass surrounding her.

The whirring sound was behind her. Metal-on-metal screeches pierced the air, moving toward her. The grass stalks bent, touching her feet.

In a burst of adrenaline, Shelby ducked beneath the water and threaded her way deeper into the marsh. She moved as fast as she could to get away from the looming hulk of the skiff, plowing toward her through the marsh, pushing the skiff beneath it.

The adrenaline and her strength waning, she barely stayed ahead of the skiff being bull-dozed through the grass.

Shelby surfaced for air, so tired she barely had the energy to breathe. It would be so much easier to die.

Holding onto several stalks, she turned to face her death.

The engine cut off. Two lights shined out over the marsh. Another light blinked to life, the beam sweeping over the skiff's hull and the surrounding area.

As the beam neared Shelby, she sank beneath the surface and shifted the reeds enough to cover her head. The beam shone across her position.

Shelby froze. For a long moment, the ray held steady. If it didn't move on soon, she'd be forced to surface to breathe.

When she thought her lungs would burst, the beam shifted past.

Shelby tilted her head back, let her nose and mouth rise to the surface and breathed in.

The light swept back her way so fast she didn't have time to duck lower. Shelby stiffened, her pulse pounding through her veins and throbbing in her head.

Before the light reached her, it snapped off.

She dared to raise her head out of the water enough to clear her ears.

"She has to be dead," a voice said.

Through the reeds, Shelby could just make out two silhouettes between the headlights of the airboat.

"We need to flip the skiff and make sure," a lower voice said.

"I'm not getting in that water to flip no skiff. I saw four alligators earlier."

"You don't see them now," the man with the lower voice argued.

"Exactly why I'm not getting in the water. You don't know where they are in the dark. If you want to check, you get in."

After a pause, the man with the deep voice said. "You're right. Alligators are sneaky bastards."

"Damn right," his partner agreed. "Besides, that woman's dead."

"And if she's not?"

The flashlight blinked on again, the beam directed at the skiff. "She'd better be," the guy with the higher voice said. "Do you see the lettering on the side of that boat?"

"S-h-e-r..." Low-voice man spoke each letter out loud and then paused.

"It spells sheriff," the other guy finished.

"Fuck," low-voice man swore. "We killed a goddamn sheriff?"

"Yeah." The flashlight blinked off. "Let's get the fuck out of here."

The airboat engine revved, and the huge fan on the back of the craft whirred to life. The airboat backed off the skiff and turned, the lights sweeping over Shelby's position.

She sank below the water's surface, the sound of the airboat rumbling in her ears.

Soon, the sound faded.

Shelby bobbed to the surface. The airboat was

gone, and with it, the bright lights. Clouds scudded across the night sky, alternately blocking and revealing a fingernail moon. When it wasn't shrouded in clouds, it glowed softly, turning the inky black into indigo blue.

Her strength waning and her vision fading in and out of a gray mist, Shelby couldn't think past the throbbing in her head.

Out of the haze, the man's comment about alligators surfaced.

She hadn't escaped death by drowning only to become dinner to a hungry reptile.

Somehow, she managed to push her way back through the marsh grass to the mangled hull of the skiff, now crushed low and only a couple of inches above the water's surface. Shelby tried to pull herself up onto the side of the slick metal hull. With nothing to grab hold of, she had no leverage, nor did she have the strength.

Swimming around to the stern, she stepped onto the motionless propeller. With her last ounce of strength and energy, she pushed upward and flopped her body onto the hull. Her forehead bounced against the metal, sending a sharp pain through her already aching head.

Though the clouds chose that moment to clear and let the moon shine down on the bayou, Shelby succumbed to darkness.

CHAPTER 2

REMY MONTAGNE PACED the war room in Hank Patterson's basement. "I've contacted all the men on my list of candidates. They're all on their way here from the airport." He glanced down at his watch. "They should arrive in thirty minutes."

Hank, an ex-Navy SEAL and the founder of the protection service Brotherhood Protectors, sat beside his computer guy, Axel Svenson, also ex-Navy SEAL, at the large conference table.

"Good," Hank said. "Which means we need to nail down a location for the new regional office. I didn't think it would take this long to find and close on a facility. Every building we've considered in New Orleans and Baton Rouge was snapped up before we could get our offer in."

"I know I'm the new guy," Remy stopped and faced Hank, "and you've been at this for a while, but why are you focusing on the big cities when the smaller towns have been working for you?"

Hank tipped his head toward the man beside him. "Swede and I thought it might be better to have at least one of our teams based out of a major city."

"Well, it doesn't seem to be working for you. I know of an empty boat factory building in Bayou Mambaloa that you could probably get for a song. It's not that far from the Big Easy. I could go out there, scout the location and send you all the details and pictures. I could probably hunt up local contractors who could bid on the renovations we'll need."

Hank's brow rose, a slow grin spreading across his face. "Would Bayou Mambaloa be the same place you visited a month ago? Your hometown?"

Remy shrugged. "Yes, sir. It's only forty minutes outside the city. Far enough to be out of the drive-by shootings and crushing traffic, yet near enough we can deploy agents to clients in New Orleans or Baton Rouge. It's closer to a major metropolitan area than Eagle Rock, Montana, is to any city of significant size."

Swede's lips twisted, his white-blond brows rising toward his shock of white-blond hair. "He's got a point. We don't lack for work out in the wilds of Montana. It might be better if we're not positioned in the city but poised on the outskirts." Hank's guru grinned. "Unless you just wanted a good excuse to mix business with pleasure during visits to New Orleans."

Remy's memories surfaced of eating his way through the French Quarter with various versions of etouffee, jambalaya and gumbo, each more delicious than the last. He never passed on a chance to eat beignets, drink espresso and people-watch at Café Dumonde.

Sure, it would be nice to have all that at your fingertips, but at what cost? Traffic was terrible, and people were constantly in bidding wars over buildings that were crazy expensive.

"Though I've enjoyed each of my visits to New Orleans," Hank said, "eating beignets for breakfast every day was not my primary reason for basing operations in the city."

He drew in a deep breath, his brow knitting. "However, a quieter location would be better to position our operation in the south. So, Bayou Mambaloa, huh?" He cocked an eyebrow and met Remy's gaze, a smile tugging at his lips. "I thought you didn't want to move back home."

Remy lifted a shoulder and let it fall. "Being back a few weeks ago reminded me of my adventures in the bayou—the festivals, the floating parades and the food." And Shelby Taylor, the woman he'd hooked up with for one night on his vacation and had sworn to himself it wouldn't be the last time.

Not knowing if or when he'd ever be back or if

she'd truly only wanted just a one-night stand, he hadn't called her.

On his way out of his hometown of Bayou Mambaloa, he'd stopped at Broussard Country Store, the business Shelby's older sister, Chrissy, and her husband, Alan, owned and operated while raising five little boys. He'd left his contact information with Chrissy in case she wanted to keep in touch for old-time's sake.

Truthfully, he'd hoped she'd pass it on to Shelby and that Shelby would call him.

She hadn't.

Instead, he'd looked up the number for Broussard Country Store in Bayou Mambaloa, saved it in his contacts list and even dialed it. When a woman had answered who'd sounded just like Shelby, he'd hung up.

What was he going to say to Shelby's sibling, the girl he'd dated all through high school?

Hey, Chrissy, I had sex with your little sister and would like to get her phone number to see if she wants to do it again?

Oh, hell no. Two and a half weeks had passed at that point. Shelby had insisted on once and done. No regrets. No strings.

If he wanted to start something again, he had to do it in person.

So, another week had passed since that stormy

night on the bayou. The memory of her naked body seared into his memory hadn't faded at all.

He woke from dreams of making love with her, hard as stone. The longer he remained in Montana, the more frustrated he became. He was ready to chuck everything and return to Bayou Mambaloa on the next plane out of Bozeman.

He hadn't realized he'd been pacing again until he looked up and caught Hank's gaze.

Hank grinned. "What's her name?"

Remy's cheeks heated. "I don't know what you're talking about," he hedged, looking away.

Hank chuckled. "Right." He pushed to his feet. "Okay, then. You'll conduct the reconnaissance mission to find our building location. We'll also need lodging for your guys as they come on board. Is Bayou Mambaloa big enough to house eight to ten guys at any one time?"

"There's the Bayou Hotel, several bed and breakfasts and, if I remember correctly, there was an old boarding house close to the boat factory where the workers used to live," Remy's eyes narrowed as he tried to recall its exact location. He hadn't passed it when he'd been in town. "I'm not sure what shape it's in."

"We've had good luck basing our Colorado and Yellowstone field offices in lodge basements or barns, setting aside several rooms for our people. It's worked out well for the guys, giving them time to decide where they want to live. Like Bayou Mambaloa, Eagle Rock has a lodge and bed and breakfasts. Sadie and I have had some of our Montana team stay with us here at the White Oak Ranch on a temporary basis. We also have a hunting cabin and a fishing cabin we've housed guys in."

Remy nodded. "We'll need alternative office space and living quarters until we can secure our own buildings. I'll check into what's available and let you know."

Hank nodded. "Are you comfortable taking the lead with the new location?"

Remy nodded. "I am, especially if it's in my old stomping grounds. I know a lot of the people who still live there."

"I'd go with you, but I promised Sadie I'd escort the kids out to LA, where she's on location for her latest movie."

Remy couldn't get over the fact Hank had married the mega-star, Sadie McClain. How lucky could a guy get?

Hank continued, "The rest of the team are gainfully employed at the moment. Joseph Kuntz—his call sign is Kujo—might free up in the next week. He helped set up the Colorado location with Jacob Cogburn."

Remy grinned. "Kujo and Cog. They were practically legends in my old team."

Hank frowned. "Watch it. You're making me feel old."

Remy laughed. "No older than I am. I'm fucking retired." His smile faded. "I never thought much about what I'd do after separating from the Navy until about six months from my official retirement date."

Swede snorted. "At least you knew ahead of time so you could prepare. Some of us were kicked to the curb by medical boards for injuries sustained in the line of duty."

"You're right," Remy nodded. He knew a lot of guys who'd never made it to retirement, and some had never made it home, except in a body bag. "I was lucky to live to retirement with few lasting reminders of war wounds sustained defending our country." At least physical wounds. PTSD was real and haunted him on occasion.

Remy glanced at his watch, surprised at what time it was. "We should go through the dossiers of the guys who'll be here shortly at least one more time. I mean, I know the Navy guys and a couple of the Delta Force men, but not everyone. Where did you get the names of the guys coming off active duty and those who've been out for a while?"

Hank settled back in his seat and turned toward the large computer screen hanging on the wall. "I have sources," he answered.

"Word gets around," Swede said. "Guys who've

recently separated stay in touch with their old teams."

Hank nodded. "Their former teammates like to know there's a place for them on the 'outside.' They can choose to continue to use their training, protecting or rescuing individuals from natural disasters or dangerous, man-made situations. I get calls from them or their commanding officers when they're about to leave the only job they've ever known."

"I know I was glad to connect," Remy said. "Twenty years in the Navy leaves its mark on a person. I barely remember how to be a civilian. When someone complains that their air conditioner doesn't blow cool enough, I fight the urge to tell them to join the Army, Navy, Marines or Air Force. Stand outside in one-hundred and twenty degrees with your feet baking in your boots, and then tell me your AC isn't cool enough."

"Only seven percent of the US population have ever served in the military," Hank said. "So many of them don't understand or realize just how insulated they are against the horrors of war."

"The dichotomy of everyday life from military to civilian never ceases to amaze me." Remy shook his head. "While they're standing in line for a movie, our soldiers and sailors are dodging bullets or mortar rounds. While they're struggling with what fast-food restaurant to grab food for the family on the way home from work, our guys might be up to their elbows in sand or stuck on a ship or in a submarine for months, away from their families, missing their kids' birthdays and ball games."

"It's an adjustment coming back," Swede said. He tapped his fingers on the keyboard in front of him, and a face popped up on the large screen. "Your future team should be arriving soon. Let's get familiar with who they are and what skills they bring to the table." He nodded toward the first image. "Gerard Guidry, Marine Force Recon, medical boarded out for injury sustained in a firefight."

Remy studied the man's intense face. He looked like he could chew nails for fun. "Gerard is a two-time purple heart and bronze star recipient. Deployed eleven times in his thirteen years on active duty, he served as a team medic. He grew up in Lafayette, Louisiana. Almost didn't get him when I told him we'd base out of Louisiana."

"Did you ask him why?" Hank asked.

"Yeah. He didn't say."

Swede brought up the next image. "Lucas LaBlanc."

"LeBlanc was Delta Force, a Medal of Honor recipient and is highly skilled on numerous weapons and hand-to-hand combat," Remy said.

"Reason for leaving the military?" Hank asked.

"His mother, and only living relative, was diagnosed with pancreatic cancer," Remy said. "He got out to be with her the last few months of her life and didn't go back into the Army after she died."

Hank's lips pressed together. "That's hard."

Remy was lucky both his parents were still alive and loving retirement in Florida. He nodded to Swede.

Swede loaded the next image of a blond-haired, green-eyed man with a boy-next-door look.

"Beau Boyette, former Army Airborne Ranger. Only survivor in a Black Hawk helicopter crash. Lost his entire squad. Though he broke a few bones and suffered a concussion, he lived. He was treated for survivor's guilt and PTSD but ended up leaving the military anyway."

"Losing your entire team is hard to work past," Hank said. "Our guys find camaraderie in the Brotherhood. Hopefully, Boyette will as well."

"He needs the work and has skills we can use," Remy said. "He grew up in Metairie, a suburb of New Orleans, so he'll be close to home."

"Is his family still there?" Hank asked.

Remy nodded. "His mother and sister."

"Good. More of a support system nearby." He nodded to Swede.

The next image appeared of a dark-haired, dark-eyed man with a smoldering frown denting his smooth forehead.

"This is one I added to the list you gave me. Rafael Romero, aka Romeo," Remy said with a smile that quickly slipped as he continued. "Navy SEAL. We served on the same team for a few years. Excellent marksman and demolitions guy. He left the military a couple of years ago to get married and settle down with his wife and start a family."

"Nice. A married man," Hank said.

Remy shook his head. "The wedding never happened. The bride ran off with the maid of honor the night before the wedding. Romeo didn't take it well. We all wanted him to come back to the unit. Instead, he signed on with a black ops security firm and shipped out to Afghanistan. He's been a lot of places since, but I talked him into coming back to the States."

"I bet he has some stories to tell," Swede murmured as he brought up the next image of a man with dark hair, dark eyes and an angular face.

Remy tipped his head toward the photo. "Valentine Vachon. Navy SEAL. Goes by Val. Trained in Mississippi water warfare. Because of his skills with watercraft, he deployed to Africa, the Amazon and Central America, primarily working extraction operations. Left the Navy when they tried to get him to go back to San Diego to train Navy SEAL candidates at BUD/S. He told the powers-that-be he didn't have the patience to babysit kids."

Hank's brow furrowed. "He does realize he'll be working with clients of all ages, doesn't he?"

Remy grinned. "He does. He said he really got out

of the Navy because the training position was to keep him in line. The missions were getting too political for him. They tied his hands once too often, to the point it was putting his team and himself in more danger than was necessary. They cared more about politics than his team." He glanced at his watch. "The guys should be here any moment."

Swede popped up the next image of a man with sandy-blond hair and blue eyes.

"Landry Laurent," Remy said quickly. "Navy SEAL. Only son of Tristan Laurent."

Hank's eyes narrowed. "Tristan Laurent of the Laurent Foundation. One of the richest men in the world."

Remy nodded. "Landry rejected his father's request to join the family's multi-billion-dollar business. He joined the Navy to prove to his father and himself that he could make it on his own. And he has. Unlike the other guys, he's not joining Brotherhood Protectors so much for gainful employment. He's good at investments and has his own stash of cash, earning interest and dividends. He's joining Brotherhood Protectors because he likes making a difference."

"Admirable," Hank said. "Is that also the reason he left the military?"

Remy nodded. "He didn't feel he was making a difference anymore in the military. He did ask that he not be assigned to protect a child."

Hank's lips twisted. "Good to know. I take it he's never had any of his own?"

"No," Remy said. "His words were, 'I don't much care for them.'"

A speaker crackled overhead, and Sadie's voice came through. "Remy and Hank, your guests just pulled through the front gate."

"Thank you, dear," Hank called out.

"You're quite welcome," she said.

Swede loaded three images onto the big screen.

Remy nodded. "The last three are Sinclaire Sevier, aka Sin, Jacques Jardine and Xavier Xander. Sin was Delta Force." Remy nodded to the picture at the center. "Jacques Jardine, Navy SEAL, and Xavier Xander, also a Navy SEAL. Plus me, that makes ten new members of the Brother Hood Protectors, if they all make it out to Louisiana without changing their minds."

Hank held out his hand to Remy. "Great job recruiting qualified candidates."

"Thank you, sir," Remy said, his chest swelling just a little. "I was fortunate to get them all to agree to come for an introductory meeting here at the ranch. They're excited to meet you. You're practically a legend among special operations teams."

"Is that because I've been around for a while, aka old?" Hank said with a twist of his lips.

Remy chuckled. "Not at all. The fact that you've built a successful business in the States, manning it with former spec ops personnel, gives us hope for a real future."

"I need their skills. *People* need their skills. I just facilitate connecting the skilled operators with the people who need them."

"It's commendable," Remy said. "We can help others using the skills we learned on active duty. All that training isn't going to waste."

"Exactly." Hank clapped his hands together. "Let's go up and meet our new Bayou Brotherhood team in person."

Remy's brow wrinkled. "Bayou Brotherhood?"

"I like the ring of it. And if you have your way, we'll be setting up operations in a bayou."

Remy's chest swelled. Coming to work for Hank and the Brotherhood Protectors was an honor. He'd never thought Hank would put him in charge of standing up a new regional office. The challenge was at once overwhelming and exciting. The team he'd assembled of his peers would make his job easy as the man in charge of the satellite branch. Each man had the skills needed and the drive and determination to make any assignment a success.

Remy and Swede followed Hank out of the basement of Hank and Sadie's ranch house. They'd built the house with the basement beneath it with Hank's brainchild in mind. They lived comfortably in the spacious house above, and Hank had quick and easy access to the Brotherhood Protectors' headquarters, computers and armory.

If Remy hoped to be as successful, he would have to get started. It took time to build or renovate what he'd need. In the meantime, he'd have to find a place to rent.

And hopefully, run into Shelby. He wondered if she thought much about that night they'd sheltered from the storm in that old fishing shack. Did she remember it as vividly as he did? Did it linger in her memories and dreams?

He'd find out soon enough. If all went well, he'd be down there within the next week.

The two SUVs Hank had sent out to pick up the men from the airport pulled up to the ranch house and parked.

Doors opened. The drivers were two men from Hank's team, Chuck Johnson and Brandon Rayne, "Boomer" to his friends. The passengers, Remy's future team, stepped out and stretched, their gazes taking in the mountains, the ranch house and people standing on the front porch.

Remy, Swede and Hank descended the steps together and shook hands with each man, introducing themselves.

Once they'd made their rounds, Hank turned toward the house. "Come meet my beautiful wife. You might recognize her if you're much of a movie buff." He strode up the steps and slipped his arm around the beautiful blond movie star. "Guys, this is my wife, Sadie McClain." He turned to Sadie. "These men are the newest of the Brotherhood Protectors."

She gave them her megawatt smile that had earned her worldwide acclaim and affection. "Welcome to White Oak Ranch and the Brotherhood Protectors. Come in. Come in. I have lemonade prepared for those who care for it."

"And I have beer for those who don't," Hank said with a wink.

They filed into the house, with Remy bringing up the rear with Romeo.

"Thanks for thinking of me," Romeo said. "I was ready to come back to the States months ago; I just wasn't sure where I'd fit in."

Remy clapped a hand on his shoulder. "From what I can tell so far, you're in the right place. Hank's a good guy, and he's made quite a name for himself with the work he's done."

"So I've heard."

As they stepped through the door, Remy's cell phone chirped in his pocket. He pulled it out and frowned down at the name on the screen, his pulse kicking into high gear.

Broussard Country Store.

"Excuse me," he said to Romeo. "I'll be right there. I need to take this call."

Why would he be receiving a call from Broussard Country Store? Could it be that Shelby had asked her sister if he'd left his contact information? Had Chrissy given her the number just now? Or was it Chrissy 'staying in touch'?

He swiped his finger across the screen and stepped back out onto the porch. "This is Remy."

"Remy, it's Chrissy Broussard, uh Taylor, from Bayou Mambaloa."

His heart sank. He'd held out hope that Shelby would be the one to place this call. "Hey, Chrissy, it's good to hear from you." And it was good to hear from her. She might have insight into what Shelby was up to and how she'd felt after their night in the bayou.

"It's Shelby." Chrissy's voice broke on a sob. "I… she…needs you."

CHAPTER 3

Remy gripped the cell phone tighter. "Chrissy, take a deep breath and tell me what's going on."

Chrissy inhaled, her breath catching several times before she spoke again. "She's in the hospital in New Orleans. I want to be with her, but I can't leave the boys, and Alan can't manage the store and the boys by himself. I wouldn't have called, but the hospital staff notified me that someone entered her room last night and tried to smother her."

Remy nearly dropped the phone. "What the hell? Shelby's in the hospital? Why? Start from the beginning."

"I'm sorry. I'm just so beside myself. Shelby's my only sibling. My only family. I don't know what I'd do…"

"Chrissy, pull yourself together and tell me what you know, from the start."

She sobbed again, then sniffed loudly in Remy's ear. "I got a call from the sheriff's department last night. The sheriff said Shelby was airlifted to a hospital in New Orleans. He said, J.D. LaDue—you know, the man who rented you his fishing shack…?"

"Right, I know who J.D. is." Remy's impatience was evident in how sharply he'd spoken. He spoke in a softer tone. "What about him?"

"The sheriff said Shelby was out in the bayou looking for evidence of a drug run transfer. When she didn't report in before dark, the sheriff got worried and drove to the marina to look for her and the department's skiff." Her breath hitched.

"What happened?" Remy barked into the phone.

"She wasn't there," Chrissy cried. "As the sheriff turned to leave, he spotted a small boat coming in and stopped to see if it was Shelby."

"And?"

"It wasn't, but it was," Chrissy wailed.

"Explain," Remy urged, wishing he was there to comfort the hysterical woman with a hug.

"It was J.D. LaDue. He had Shelby in his boat. She was unconscious, barely breathing," Chrissy sucked in a breath and continued, "The sheriff got an ambulance there in less than five minutes, but she didn't come to and hasn't woken up since J.D. brought her in."

"Did J.D. say what happened?"

"He told the sheriff he found her little boat

upside-down in the water with Shelby sprawled across the hull, out cold."

"Any visible wounds?" Remy asked, his heart in his throat.

"She had a gash on her forehead and bruises on her arms," Chrissy said. "I stayed with her for a few hours last night but had to get back to the boys." She sobbed again. "I should've stayed all night. It was after I left that someone came in and tried to smother her."

"What the hell?" Remy exclaimed.

"I know," Chrissy said. "I should've stayed. The nurses said they'd responded to someone coding in another room. While they were working on him, Shelby's alarms went off. Her heart had stopped."

Remy's heartbeat came to an abrupt stop and then pounded to catch up. He gripped the phone hard. "Is she—"

Chrissy kept talking as if she hadn't heard his words. "When the nurses hurried to her room, someone wearing a black ski mask pushed past them and ran for the stairwell. While one nurse alerted security, the others found Shelby lying in her bed, a pillow over her face, her rolling table lowered on top of it to hold it in place." Chrissy sobbed. "Someone tried to kill my sister!"

Remy clung to the word 'tried.' "But she's okay, right? They got to her in time?" He held his breath.

"They had to…jumpstart…her heart…two times

before…it started beating on its own." Chrissy was sobbing again.

In the background, Remy could hear a man's voice say, "Give it to me."

A moment later, that man spoke clearly, "Remy, this is Alan. My wife seems to think you can help her sister. But from what I understand, you're clear across the country in Montana. What she needs is a bodyguard sitting with her until she wakes up and can tell the police who did this to her. The hospital's security is understaffed, as is the New Orleans Police Department. Chrissy's afraid whoever tried to kill her will try again. I don't want her there if that someone comes back. She's not trained in self-defense, and they don't allow guns in the hospital."

Remy spun and pushed through the front door of the ranch house. "Text me the name of the hospital and the room number. I'll get someone there within the next hour to keep watch over her until I can get there."

"Will do," Alan said. "I'd go myself, but my parents are out of town, and they can't take the boys. One of my refrigerators decided to quit, and I have a truckload of perishables to be unloaded."

"I'll take care of her," Remy said. "I'll get back to you when I've firmed up my plans. You take care of your family."

"I'll let Chrissy know you're on it," Alan said. "Thanks, Remy."

Remy ended the call and followed the sound of voices and laughter emanating from the large kitchen.

When he entered, all faces turned toward him.

Hank held his son, McClain, in his arms while his daughter, Emma, clung to one of his legs. "What's wrong?" he asked, handing the boy to Sadie.

She took McClain and reached for Emma's hand.

"I have a situation in New Orleans and Bayou Mambaloa that I'll need your help to handle in the short run until I can get down there."

Hank lifted his head toward the living room. "Now's as good a time as any for your new team to see how we do things in the Brotherhood Protectors. Let's take it to the war room."

Swede was already on his way out of the kitchen with Remy on his heels.

When Swede reached the hidden door to the staircase leading down to the basement headquarters, he opened a panel, pressed his thumb to the print scanner and bent his tall frame to the eye reader. The door slid open. As he descended the staircase, motion detectors switched on lights, and soon, the entire basement was lit.

Hank fell in beside Remy. "Give me the Sitrep."

"Shelby Taylor was found unconscious on her overturned boat in the bayou. They airlifted her to a New Orleans hospital. She hasn't regained consciousness. Late last night, someone entered her room and tried to smother her—and almost succeeded. The nurses were able to revive her, but they don't have the staffing to guard her while she's there."

"I have an old Navy buddy who lives in New Orleans. Tyson King. We called him Tiger." Hank shot a glance across the room. "Swede—"

"On it." Swede's fingers flew across the keyboard. He brought up a contacts list, keyed in Tyson King and video-called the number listed.

After the phone rang four times, the large screen at the end of the conference room blinked, and a man's face appeared. He had shaggy salt-and-pepper hair and a short beard of the same color. He appeared to be seated in an outdoor lounge chair with a beer in one hand. "Hank, you old bastard, are you having a party without me?"

Hank grinned. "Looks like you're having one of your own."

"A party of one." He held up his beer in salute. "To what do I owe this occasion of your call?"

"Are you in New Orleans?"

"I sure as hell am not on a beach in the Bahamas. It's hot as fuck, and I'm melting in the humidity. Sure could use a trip to Montana about now." Tiger grinned. "What can I do you for?"

Hank's grin straightened. "Need a favor."

All humor left Tiger's face. "Name it."

"Got a young lady in a hospital in your lovely city.

Someone tried to smother her last night. I need someone to keep an eye on her until my man Remy Montagne can get down there to take over." Hank draped an arm over Remy's shoulders.

"Is she pretty?" Tiger asked.

Remy stiffened. The man was older than him, but not much. And he was still in good shape, even if his hair needed a good cut.

"Just kidding," Tiger said. "I won't cut in on another man's woman."

Remy almost said *she's not my woman* but kept his mouth shut. Better to let Tiger think she was his to keep him from hitting on her when she finally woke.

"Where can I find this sweet thing?" Tiger asked.

Remy hesitated.

Hank grinned. "You can trust Tiger. He's a big talker, but he's actually afraid of women."

Tiger's eyebrows descended. "Don't know where you got that idea. I love women."

"If they're under eight years old or over eighty. Anything in between, you run from."

Tiger snorted. "I call it self-preservation."

Remy gave him the name of the hospital and Shelby's room number. "Her name is Shelby Taylor. She's a sheriff's deputy."

"So don't pull any fast ones, right, or she'll serve my balls on a platter?" Tiger laughed at his own words. "Got it. I can be there in twenty minutes, depending on traffic."

"I'll have Remy on a plane as soon as possible. He should be there no later than tomorrow morning," Hank said. "Earlier if I can arrange it."

"I'm good for as long as you need me," Tiger said. "Out here."

"Out here," Hank echoed.

The big screen went black.

Hank turned to Swede. "I'll need—"

"I've put our pilot on alert. He'll have the flight plan recorded, the plane fueled, and the pre-flight checklist complete in under an hour."

Hank grinned. "That gives us time to drive Remy to the airport in Bozeman." He turned to Remy.

"I can have my bags packed in ten minutes." He turned to the men he'd selected for his team. "Welcome to Brotherhood Protectors. I'm glad you made it here and agreed to sign on to this organization. Are you all ready to go to work?"

"Yes, sir!" the men shouted like basic trainees to their drill instructor.

Remy grinned. "Good. So am I. I'd hoped to spend time with each of you to get to know you and answer whatever questions you might have, but Hank will do a much better job as he's been at this a lot longer than I have. I only have a couple of weeks on you, and I haven't had my first assignment."

"You just got it," Hank said softly. "Shelby Taylor needs protection."

Remy gave his new boss a crooked grin. "You're right."

"How do you know whether or not she can pay for the protection?" Lucas asked.

Hank opened his mouth to address the man's question.

Remy held up his hand before Hank could say anything. "Can I answer that?"

Hank dipped his head.

"I spoke with some of the Brotherhood Protectors before I agreed to hire on with Hank. They all had the same things to say. Hank's great to work with. It's a team where everyone helps where needed. The best part is that we take on cases whether they can pay or not. Bottom line is we help people. Hank and Sadie will fund where others are unable to pay for our services. They want every client who needs help to get it, regardless of their financial situation."

Hank nodded. "You'd be surprised how many people who *can* afford to pay donate to our organization to help others. Our good deeds are noticed and rewarded so that we can continue to help others."

"I know you came today for some kind of orientation," Remy said. "I wanted you all to meet and get to know each other because we'll be starting up a new branch of the Brotherhood Protectors in Louisiana. We don't yet have a location for our office, but I'll be working on that as well. You're all scheduled to come on board in the next few weeks. Between me, Hank and Swede, we hope to have something set up by then."

"I'm ready to deploy—go now. I came here with my go bag," Gerard said. "I don't need a fancy office to get started."

"Same," Lucas said.

"Count me in," came a chorus of responses from the others.

Remy's heart swelled. "That's great. I'm glad you're as excited as I am to get started. But for now, I'd like to keep it simple. Gerard, if you're serious, I'd like to take you along in case I need backup. As soon as I secure a location to set up shop, I'll send for the rest of you. You'll want to drive down with your own vehicles. Speaking of which…" He turned to Hank.

Hank opened his mouth, but Swede was first to speak.

"There will be a rental vehicle waiting at the airport for you," Swede said from where he sat at his computer.

Hank grinned. "I swear he—"

"—reads your mind?" Swede finished. "Damn right, I do. And right now, you're thinking you need to have someone fuel up one of the SUVs that brought these men here so it can head back to the airport in Bozeman."

Hank's lips twisted. "Again, he's reading my mind."

Swede nodded. "You might not have noticed that

Chuck left the war room a few minutes ago to put fuel in the SUV he drove. He'll drive Remy and Gerard to the airport."

"I'll pack," Remy said. He turned to the others with an apologetic shrug. "I guess I'll see you all soon."

"Don't worry about them. Swede and I will bring them up to speed," Hank said. "Go."

Remy sprinted up the stairs leading out of the basement. His gear was in one of the guest bedrooms. When he'd separated from the Navy, he'd sold almost everything in his apartment, packed what he could fit in his truck and donated the rest to a shelter. A week's worth of clothes, his rifle and handgun, boots, running shoes and his Navy dress uniform were all he'd brought with him.

He hadn't wanted to move furniture across the country as most of it was second-hand and not worth dragging into his new life as a civilian. He'd figured when he got where he was going, he'd furnish his place a piece at a time. Now that he was retired from the military, he had the rest of his life to establish a home. He was looking forward to buying a house where he could change the color of the paint on the walls or build a deck out back.

Because he'd deployed so often, he hadn't felt the need to own a house. Renting an apartment had meant he could button up and leave at a moment's notice, and someone else would maintain the building and yard. He hadn't lived in a house with a yard since he'd left home twenty years before.

Call him crazy, but Remy looked forward to home ownership with grass he had to mow. At the back of his mind, he'd even had thoughts of finding someone to share that house and yard. Granted, he'd even considered getting a dog if the right person didn't come along.

Then, on his fishing vacation in Bayou Mambaloa, he'd run across Shelby Taylor, adrift in a boat with a dead motor, rain pouring down on her.

With a storm bearing down on them, he'd taken her to the fishing hut he'd rented for the week. The storm outside had nothing on the storm of passion that had consumed them inside the hut.

Now, Shelby lay unconscious in a hospital after she'd had possibly two attempts on her life. One that put her in the hospital and another to finish the job while she lay unable to defend herself.

Anger burned deep in Remy's gut. He couldn't imagine anyone wanting to hurt Shelby. Then again, she was a sheriff's deputy. She'd been in the bayou when they'd found her. Someone must think she'd witnessed something worth killing her to keep her from reporting it to her sheriff.

Remy jammed his clothes into his duffel bag and hurried into the adjoining bathroom to collect his comb, shaving gear and toothbrush. He slid his toiletries into a shaving kit and shoved the kit into the duffel bag.

Lastly, he removed the handgun from the nightstand where he'd kept it since he'd arrived, slid his arms into his shoulder holster and tucked the gun into place. He pulled on his leather jacket, settled his favorite ball cap on his head and slung the duffel bag over one shoulder. He grabbed his rifle case and left the bedroom.

Hank met him in the living room with a gym bag.

"Are you coming with us?" Remy asked.

Hank laughed. "I would, but I promised Sadie that the kids and I would accompany her to LA for the premier of her latest movie release. She supports me in all I do with the Brotherhood Protectors. I want to support her in her amazing work as an actor. She's a gifted performer, and I'm proud she chose me to share her life."

The few weeks he'd stayed with Hank and Sadie, he'd witnessed the love the couple had for each other and their children. "You're a lucky man, Hank."

Hank nodded. "Don't I know it." He walked with Remy out of the house to the waiting SUV.

Chuck Johnson, the ex-Navy SEAL who'd also worked for the FBI after he'd left the Navy, stood beside the driver's door.

Gerard opened the hatch. "I already stowed my gear."

Remy tossed his duffel into the back and laid his rifle case beside it. He reached up to close the hatch.

Hank stopped him with a hand on his arm. "Take this bag with you. I've loaded it with some things you might need, or maybe not, but you'll have them in case you do." He handed Remy the bag.

"What's in it?" Remy asked.

"Communications equipment, a tracking device and tracker chips, zip-ties, rope, carabiners, bear spray and other stuff."

"Bear spray?" Remy laughed. "As far as I know, we don't have bears in the bayou."

"No, but it's pepper spray, and maybe it will help keep the alligators away or any human aggressors."

"I read that pepper spray is not as effective on alligators," Remy said. "

Gerard chimed in. "Because of their thick hides, the pepper spray doesn't penetrate as well. I must have read the same article. Anything about alligators catches my attention. I used to help my uncle remove alligators out of residential areas in Lafayette."

"I knew there was a reason we needed you on the team." Remy tossed the equipment bag into the rear of the vehicle. "Thanks, Hank. I'm sure we'll need all of this and then some."

"As soon as you find a place to set up shop, we'll order what you need," Hank said. "In the meantime, let us know if you want anything. We can get things shipped quickly."

"Thanks." Remy held out his hand.

Hank took it in a firm grip and met his gaze. "I hope Shelby recovers quickly. And just as important, I hope you find who was responsible in the first place."

Remy's jaw hardened. "We will."

Remy wanted to be there when she woke. The sooner she could tell them what had happened, the better.

Until they found who'd attacked Shelby, she'd remain a target.

Knowing the stubborn, independent sheriff's deputy, she'd want to get right back to work. If she was still unconscious hours and maybe days after her injury, she must have suffered a concussion or some other brain injury. Surely, the doctor wouldn't clear her to return to work right away. She'd be pissed and probably try to solve her own case while off-duty.

Which would make his job more difficult. But he was up for the challenge. Remy planned on sticking to Shelby like fly paper. He'd stay with her twenty-four-seven until her attackers were caught.

Remy grinned. He'd definitely get under her skin. All that togetherness would give him a chance to get to know her better and her to get to know him. For the woman who'd insisted on only a one-night stand, she might chafe at his incessant presence. Or, she might come to the same conclusion Remy had already reached.

REMY

One night together hadn't been nearly enough.

He climbed into the front passenger seat of the SUV. Gerard sat behind him. As Chuck drove away from the ranch house, Remy looked back at the men he and Hank had chosen for the newest regional office of the Brotherhood Protectors. They'd soon become the Bayou Brotherhood Protectors, helping people in difficult situations.

His retirement from the Navy wasn't going to be all about fishing and playing golf. He had a real job that promised to keep him challenged and engaged for a very long time.

Starting with the mission of protecting Shelby Taylor.

He leaned forward in his seat, willing the SUV to go faster. The sooner they got to the airport, the sooner he'd get to Shelby.

Remy glanced at his watch. Tiger should be arriving at the hospital. If he had cell phone reception, he'd call the man for an update.

Driving through the Crazy Mountains wasn't conducive to great cell phone coverage. He wouldn't get a call through until they got closer to Bozeman.

Until then, Remy sat in tense silence, his thoughts running through every possible scenario that could be taking place at the hospital where Shelby had been taken.

Every five minutes, Remy glanced down at his cell phone, willing the NO SERVICE message to go away and several bars indicating reception to appear.

They were less than a mile outside of Bozeman when he finally had enough reception to call Tiger.

The man answered on the first ring. "Yo, Tiger speaking."

"It's Remy." His heart beat so hard that the pulse pounding in his ears made it difficult to hear. "Are you with Shelby?"

"Roger," Tiger said.

"How is she?" Remy asked, his hand tightening around the cell phone.

Tiger let out a long sigh. "Still among the living. As far as the doctor knows, she hasn't regained consciousness since they brought her here. They did a CT scan but didn't find anything."

"No brain bleeds?"

"Nothing," Tiger reported.

"Thanks for being there," Remy said. "We're almost to the airport. We'll be there as soon as we can."

"No worries," Tiger said. "I've got this for now."

"Thanks." Remy ended the call and called Broussard Country Store.

Chrissy answered on the first ring. "Broussard Country Store."

"Chrissy, it's Remy."

"Oh, thank God. I've been going out of my mind."

"We positioned a man at the hospital to keep an

eye on Shelby. His name is Tyson King. He'll be with her until I arrive. I'm almost to the airport in Bozeman, where I'll board a plane. I don't know how long the flight will take, but I'll be at the hospital by morning, though I suspect we'll get there sooner. Either way, someone will be with her until she's released."

"Thank you," Chrissy said, her voice a whisper of relief. "J.D. LaDue is running a bag of her clothes and shoes into New Orleans for when they release her from the hospital. When you see Shelby, give her my love."

"Yes, ma'am."

"And Remy?" Chrissy continued. "For what it's worth, she's been acting weird since you left. Whatever you two did out there in the bayou during that insane storm left a mark on her."

"What did she say?" Remy asked.

"Not a damned thing," Chrissy said. "And she usually tells me everything."

Remy let go of a silent sigh of relief, glad Shelby hadn't told Chrissy about their lovemaking. He suspected she hadn't because he'd dated her older sister in high school. Not that he and Chrissy had gone all the way. Heavy petting was all they'd done before Chrissy had broken up with him. He couldn't imagine Shelby comparing notes on his performance with her sister.

If she'd enjoyed it even half as much as Remy had, would she still be thinking about him?

Not that making love mattered at the moment. Shelby needed to wake up and tell them she was all right.

Until that happened, anything else was inconsequential.

CHAPTER 4

TOO MANY STRESSFUL HOURS LATER, the jet landed at the closest general aviation airport to the hospital where Shelby had been taken. Night had cloaked the land long before they'd reached their destination. As they circled the airport, runway lights glowed brightly. The pilot bought them in for a smooth landing, the wheels kissing the ground with barely a bump. After taxiing for what felt like forever, the plane pulled to a stop at a Fixed Base Operator building.

Remy gathered his duffel bag, rifle case and the equipment Hank had given him. As soon as the door was opened, he leaped to the ground and hurried to the rental SUV waiting nearby on the tarmac with the back hatch open.

Remy tossed his gear into the rear. Right behind him, Gerard threw in his bag and gun case.

The attendant standing beside the car handed him the key. "The tank's full."

"Thank you." Remy took the key, slid into the driver's seat and connected his phone to the vehicle's onboard computer screen. As the pilot had been vectored in to land at the airport, Remy had entered the hospital's address into his phone's map application. He hit GO and pulled through the open gate and out onto the road.

Breaking most of the posted speed limits, he raced through the city to the hospital and parked. Gerard had his door open before Remy turned off the engine. The two men hurried into the hospital, passed the front desk and found the elevator.

So close now, Remy tapped his foot impatiently as the elevator slowly ascended to Shelby's floor. As soon as the door opened wide enough, he was out and scanning direction arrows, indicating which direction different rooms were located. Once he knew which way to go, he sprinted down the hallway, past a nurses' station and around a corner.

The man with shaggy salt-and-pepper hair he'd seen hours ago in the video call sat in a chair with his back to the wall outside one of the rooms.

As Remy approached, the man pushed to his feet, a grin spreading across his face. "You must be Remy Montagne." He held out his hand. "Hank said you'd be here about now."

"Tyson King, I presume?" Remy said as he gripped the man's hand.

"Most folks call me Tiger. Tyson sounds too uppity. And I'm anything but uppity."

Remy briefly shook the man's hand and turned to Gerard. "This is Gerard Guidry. We both work with Hank."

As Tiger shook Gerard's hand, Remy moved past them to the door to the room. "Has Miss Taylor regained consciousness?"

"No," Tiger said behind him. "The doctor was in a couple of times during the day. Her vital signs seem to be good. Her heart and lungs work like they should, but she hasn't woken up."

Remy shot a frown toward Tiger. "Was the doctor at all concerned? Do we need to get another opinion?"

Tiger shook his head. "He said she'd suffered a blow to the head. Though she doesn't have a brain bleed, it's still trauma to her brain. He seems to think it'll only be a matter of time before she comes to."

The room was shadowed, the only light coming from the hallway and the machines monitoring her heartbeat, blood pressure and pulse.

Remy's gut clenched as he stood beside the bed, staring down at a woman who'd chosen the path of law enforcement. A strong individual who had little patience for bullshit and a lot of love for her family and community.

Shelby lay as still as death against the sheets, a plain white blanket draped over her still form, her arms resting on the blanket. An IV dripped liquid through a tube into her arm, wires draped over her shoulder, disappearing beneath the hospital gown, the electrodes at one end feeding data to the monitor at the other.

Remy reached for the hand not connected to an IV and gently curled his fingers around hers. "Hey, Squirt." He half-hoped his voice would be the trigger to bring her out of the coma.

She didn't answer, and her hand remained limp in his.

"A family friend stopped by last night to drop off a bag of Miss Taylor's clothes and shoes. The uniform they took off her was soaked in swamp water." He pointed to a closet. "I put the bag of clean clothes in that closet."

"Thanks," Remy said. He hoped Shelby would get to wear the clothes sooner rather than later.

"If you don't need me, I'll head out," Tiger said. "You have my number. I'm only twenty minutes away."

"I'll keep that in mind." Remy released Shelby's hand and shook Tiger's. "Thank you for getting here so quickly."

"Anytime. Any friend of Hank's is a friend of mine." He nodded to Gerard. "Let me know if you need a place to stay while you're in the city. I have a couple of spare bedrooms."

"Thanks," Remy said. "We'll probably stay close to the hospital until Miss Taylor is released. Then we'll head to Bayou Mambaloa, where she lives."

Tiger shrugged. "The offer's open if you change your mind." The ex-Navy SEAL left, letting the door swing closed behind him.

Remy handed the keys to Gerard. "I saw a hotel close by. Why don't you get a room for what's left of the night? We can regroup here in the morning."

"You'll be staying here." Gerard's words were a statement, not a question.

Remy's gaze returned to Shelby. "I will."

"I can take over in the morning, or sooner, if you need me," he said.

"Thanks. Oh, and Gerard," he looked to the other man, "take my rifle and handgun into the hotel with you. I don't know how safe it is to leave anything in a vehicle around here, day or night."

"Will do," he responded. "If you're not in a hurry for me to show up in the morning, I'll see if I can find the detective in charge of whatever investigation they might be conducting into the attack on Miss Taylor."

"Please. Remember, Swede might be in Montana, but he's good at finding out things through the internet. Use his expertise."

Gerard grinned. "Nice to know he's in our corner. I'm not as tech-savvy as he is."

"You don't have to be," Remy said. "That's why we

have Swede. And if Swede isn't available, Kyla Russell out of the Yellowstone office is his backup. I'll forward both of their numbers for you to keep in your contacts list. You'll become intimately familiar with their skills as a member of the Brotherhood Protectors."

The big, former Marine Force Reconnaissance operator backed toward the door as if hospital rooms gave him the willies. "I'll be heading out then."

Remy had already turned back toward Shelby's inert form.

The door swished open and closed, leaving him alone with the woman who'd been on his mind for the past month.

Before he forgot, he forwarded the phone numbers for Swede and Kyla, sending them to Gerard.

He lifted her hand again, shocked at how fragile it felt in his. The last time he'd been with her, she'd run her strong hands all over him, kneading his flesh as he'd explored every inch of her body.

He laid her hand on the blanket, pulled a chair up to the side of the bed, and sank into it.

"This is not exactly how I envisioned 'running into you' again," he admitted, trailing his finger across her arm. "I was supposed to arrive in town looking for a building for our new office. You were supposed to drive by in your sheriff's vehicle." He smiled at the image he'd imagined so many times.

"You didn't have to go to the trouble of being hurt and in a coma to get me to come back. I was coming back anyway."

He smoothed a strand of her hair back from her forehead.

Her skin was cool to the touch.

Despite the monitor's monotonous beeping, indicating Shelby's steady heartbeat, Remy found himself leaning forward, his gaze on her chest beneath the blanket.

His breath caught and held until Shelby's chest rose ever so slightly on an indrawn breath.

He released the air in his lungs and sat back. "What happened?" he asked softly. "Who did this to you?"

She didn't answer. He didn't expect her to. But that didn't make him give up hope. As soon as she was back, they'd figure out who'd attacked her in the swamp and in the hospital and bring them down.

"I just need you to wake up, sweetheart," he said. "I've been thinking about us. I want to renegotiate our prior agreement."

Her hand twitched.

He reached out and lifted her hand in his.

"One night with you was not enough. I knew it as soon as you left the fishing shack that morning. I would've called you, but you were so insistent that you didn't want more." He pressed his lips to the back of her knuckles. "I should've called anyway. What was the worst that could happen? You could've told me to bug off. I would have, long enough to get my shit together and get back to the bayou."

Remy had heard that people in comas could hear voices; they just couldn't respond.

Shelby didn't respond, but could she hear his voice?

If she could, at least she'd know he was there, and she wasn't alone.

"The bottom line is that since the storm, I haven't stopped thinking about you. You might have walked away, or in your case, boated away, with no intention of ever starting something with me. But I'm here to tell you, I want to start something with you. I want to see where it goes. I'm finally at a place where I want to share my life with someone else. I hope that someone is you," he said softly. "What do you want?"

He paused, stared at her pale face and willed her eyes to open.

"So, are you going to play hard to get and act like we never made love in a fishing shack? I hope not. My memory of our time together is so vivid I wake up expecting to find you lying in bed beside me." He lowered his voice and scooted closer. "Your naked body pressed against mine. But I'm not just interested in making love with you. I want more. I want to spend time getting to know you. I want you to want to get to know me."

He rambled on into the wee hours of the morning

when his voice grew hoarse, and he couldn't talk anymore. Then he held her hand in his and memorized the lines in her palm.

Around four-thirty in the morning, a lab tech came through to collect a blood sample, followed by a nurse who charted Shelby's vital signs.

Even after being poked and prodded, Shelby didn't wake.

Once the medical staff left the room and silence returned, Remy closed his eyes and rested his forehead on the blanket beside Shelby's arm. Tired after being up for over twenty-four hours, he wanted to rest his eyes for a few short minutes. As soon as his eyes closed, his other senses remained on alert to footsteps in the hallway, the steady beep of the monitor, soft voices talking outside the door and every possible movement from the woman lying in the bed.

For a few minutes, Remy slept, images of Shelby lying naked on the bed in the fishing hut, smiling up at him haunting his dreams.

CHAPTER 5

Dark water.

Swirling.

Swirling.

Swimming.

Arms moving to keep her head above the surface.

Of what?

The ocean?

A lake?

A scarier thought...the bayou?

Swim harder.

Arms tired.

Water pulled at her feet, taking her deeper until her nose slipped beneath the surface. She tipped her head back, her mouth and nose breaking free of the water. She gasped, drawing air into her lungs. For several long seconds, she breathed in and out.

The darkness lightened. Black turned to gray. A

hand touched hers, gathering her fingers into a warm grip.

She clung to the hand.

"Shelby," a deep voice said in the shadows of her mind. "Shelby, honey. Please, wake up."

Wake up?

She *was* awake.

How else could she swim?

Unless…

The darkness and water were something else…

But what?

The more she tried to recall, the more her head ached.

"Open your eyes, sweetheart," a deep, sexy voice said. "You know you want to."

She was awake, wasn't she? Weren't her eyes already open? Had she slipped beneath the surface?

She tried to kick her feet to rise above the darkness. Something held her back. Her legs were trapped.

She struggled to fight free, but her muscles wouldn't cooperate.

"Wake up, Shelby," the voice sounded again, a little closer this time with warm breath fanning her cool cheek. "It's a beautiful day. Don't you want to see the sunshine?"

She nodded and frowned. How could she see the sun in the dark?

"Open your eyes," the sexy voice commanded.

"They're open," she croaked, eyes still shut.

"No, Shelby. They're closed." A hand squeezed hers gently. "Come on. You can do it. Open your eyes."

Shelby focused all her energy on her eyelids. How could they be closed when she was in the water? Or was she?

No matter how hard she concentrated, she couldn't get her eyelids to move. "Open for me," she whispered, defeated.

Something touched her face. A hand? Fingers?

One finger rested on her eyelid and slid it upward.

Bright light blinded her. She squeezed her eye closed again.

"Too bright?" the deep voice asked.

The warmth that had emanated from the man standing next to her disappeared.

A moment later, the pale gray light filtering through the seam of her closed eyelids faded to a darker color.

This time, Shelby slowly eased open her eyes and gave them a minute to focus before looking around at the sterile white walls surrounding her. She frowned. "Where am I?"

"In a hospital in New Orleans," the deep voice said.

Shelby turned to look up at the tall, broad-shouldered man with black hair and blue eyes. Her frown deepened. "Do I know you?" He seemed familiar, but she couldn't quite place him.

His brow furrowed. "Seriously? You don't know me?"

She ran her gaze over his face, across his shoulders and lower. Something about him was familiar, she just couldn't put her finger on it. Shelby pinched the bridge of her nose. "*Should* I know you?" she asked, shaking her head.

His lips pressed together. "I'm Remy."

The face...the name... She felt like she should know them.

"Remy Montagne," he said. "We grew up in the same town." He opened his mouth as if to say more, then closed it.

"Why can't I remember?" she whispered, a tear slipping from the corner of her eye.

"Do you remember who you are?" he asked.

She nodded slowly. "Shelby...Taylor."

"Do you know where you live?" Remy asked.

Her brow puckered. "Memphis? No. I left that job to go home to..." Her eyes narrowed. "Bayou Mambaloa?" A small wave of relief kept her from freaking out.

Remy nodded. "That's right. You live in Bayou Mambaloa."

She glanced around the room. "Why am I here? Was I in an accident?" The monitor's beeps increased in frequency. Shelby's cheeks flushed, and her breathing became erratic. "Is that why I can't remember you? Was anyone else hurt?"

"No one else. And you're going to be fine," Remy assured her. "You had a bump on your head and have been out for a couple of days. The doctor should be doing his morning rounds soon. He can answer all your questions better than I can."

"Why are you here?" she asked. "Where's my sister?"

"I'm here because your sister and brother-in-law can't make the trip, handle the store and take care of five children all at once. Your sister called and asked me to come keep an eye on you."

Shelby's eyes rounded. "Why you? Someone I don't know."

He touched a hand to his belly as if she'd sucker-punched him. Then he squared his shoulders. "I work with the Brotherhood Protectors, a security company that provides protection for individuals who need it."

"Wait...what?" She shook her head, making the room spin for a moment. "I need protection?"

He nodded. "Do you remember where you were before you woke up here in the hospital?"

She closed her eyes and thought back. Everything was fuzzy. "I was in the sheriff's department boat on the bayou."

He leaned forward. "Yeah. And?"

"I don't know." Shelby pinched the bridge of her nose. "There was a murder suspect who'd escaped into bayou...we were out looking for him. A storm rolled in. I remember it started raining, and my engine quit." From that point, her mind went blank. Like black, bottomless-pit blank. The harder she tried to recall anything afterward, the more it hurt.

She lay back against the pillow with her hand over her eyes. "That's it. I don't remember anything after it started raining and my engine quit." When she pulled her hand away, she stared up at Remy. "What happened after that?"

Remy's brow puckered. "Shelby, that was almost a month ago. You stayed the night in a fishing shack and...made it back to the marina the next day." He paused. "Do you remember the fishing hut?"

She narrowed her eyes, trying to remember. Alas, she couldn't. "No. Did we catch the suspect?"

Remy sighed. "Yes."

"Have I been in the hospital all this time?" she asked.

"No. You were fine after the storm. Two days ago, you were in the bayou looking for evidence of drug running." He tipped his head. "Any of that ring a bell?"

She shook her head, her breath catching in her chest. "I don't remember. Is that when the accident happened?"

Remy nodded. "Only it wasn't an accident, based on what the sheriff reported. You were found by J.D. LaDue, lying on the hull of your overturned boat, unconscious.

Shelby's heart hammered in her chest. "I dreamed I was swimming in dark water…" she whispered.

He squeezed her hand gently. "You probably were. You had to for you to get yourself up onto the hull."

A frown pinched her forehead. "How could my boat have overturned?"

"From what the sheriff described, someone rammed your boat hard enough to flip it, and then they rode up onto the hull, smashing it down in the water."

Shelby's eyes widened. "Holy shit. That was no accident."

"That's not all," he continued. "After you were brought to the hospital, someone sneaked into your room and tried to smother you."

Shelby pressed a hand to her chest, her heart beating so fast it felt like it would leap out of her chest. "Double holy shit."

"Yeah," he said, his mouth set in a grim line. "That's when your sister called me."

Shelby shook her head. "What kind of hornet's nest did I stir up?"

"That's what we all want to know," he said.

The door opened, and a man in a white coat entered. "Ah. Good." He smiled and crossed to Shelby. "I'm glad to see you're awake. I'm Doctor Richards."

The blood pressure cuff chose that moment to inflate around her arm, squeezing it hard.

Shelby lay still while the cuff did its thing, and the doctor checked her online chart. When the cuff released, she let go of the breath she'd been holding.

The doctor leaned over her and shined his penlight into her eyes. "How are you feeling?"

"Like I lost my mind," she admitted. "At least a portion of it. I can't remember what happened for—" she leaned around to look at Remy, "how long did you say?"

"Almost a month," Remy supplied.

"It's not unusual to have amnesia after a head injury," Dr. Richards said in a calm tone.

"Will I get those memories back?" Shelby asked.

"Maybe," the doctor said. "It might be temporary. As the brain heals, the memories could return."

Shelby frowned. "What if they don't?"

"Then you might have Dissociative Amnesia where your brain blocks out information surrounding the traumatic event," Dr. Richards said. "Kind of the brain's way of protecting you from reliving that trauma. In which case, you should seek a mental health provider to help you work through the trauma."

Shelby sank back against the pillow. "I don't like that I can't remember weeks of my life."

Dr. Richards smiled reassuringly. "Your family

and friends can help you fill in the gaps until your memory returns."

Shelby snorted. "Not the gap that includes who attacked me in the first place."

"True," the doctor said. "Hopefully, law enforcement can track down the attacker." He glanced at the machine readout of her blood pressure. "Your blood pressure is elevated, and your pulse is racing."

She snorted. "Wouldn't your blood pressure and pulse be wonky if you lost a month of your life?"

He nodded and pressed his stethoscope to her chest. "Take a deep breath."

Shelby inhaled and let it out slowly.

"Again," the doctor said.

She complied, her pulse slowing.

The doctor straightened. "Heart and lungs sound good. Your CT scan was clear. No brain bleeding that we could detect. Now that you're awake, we can check out the rest." He had her move her arms one at a time. Then he turned to her legs.

The doctor touched his hand to her nearest leg. "Can you feel my hand?"

"Yes," she answered, happy that she could.

He removed his hand from her leg. "Can you move your legs?"

Shelby looked up at him. "I don't know. I haven't tried."

"Start by wiggling your toes," he urged.

She lay for a long moment, concentrating on her toes. She imagined moving the toes on the right foot.

The doctor smiled. "Good. Now the other foot."

She wiggled the toes on her left foot, more confident with each accomplishment.

"Excellent," the doctor said. "Now lift your right knee."

A little less mired in the swamp of her nightmare, she lifted her right knee and then the left. "Thank God," she said as she lowered them to the mattress.

"Let's get you to sit on the edge of the bed." The doctor held out his hand.

Shelby gripped it.

Remy slipped an arm around her back. Between the two men, they had her sitting up with her legs over the side of the bed.

For a moment, her head spun. Shelby was thankful for Remy's arm behind her back for the few seconds it took to get her balance and for the spinning to diminish. Finally, she nodded. "I've got this."

The two men stepped back.

"You're doing great," the doctor said. "As soon as you can get up and walk down the hallway and back, you can go home. Someone will need to keep an eye on you for a day or two to make sure you don't have any relapses." The doctor frowned. "And to keep anyone else from attacking you." He shook his head. "I've worked in this hospital for five years and never had someone try to smother a patient." He held out his hand to Remy. "Are you her significant other?"

Before Shelby could respond, Remy said, "You could say that." He shook the doctor's hand. "I'll make sure no one tries to hurt her again."

"Good." The doctor turned back to Shelby and repeated, "A walk down the hall and back, and you can go. The nurse will give you discharge instructions and what to look out for. Give yourself a couple of weeks before you return to duty."

"A couple of weeks?" Shelby cried. "Do you know how shorthanded the sheriff's department is in Bayou Mambaloa?"

The doctor shook his head. "No, but you don't want to put anyone else at risk. No driving until after your follow-up appointment in two weeks."

"No driving?" She blew out a frustrated sigh. "What *can* I do?"

The doctor smiled. "Let your body and your brain recover. You were out for forty-eight hours. You don't want to pass out behind the wheel of a vehicle weighing more than three tons. At that point, the vehicle becomes a deadly hurtling missile, crushing anything in its path."

"Okay," Shelby said. "I get your point. No driving until I get your blessing."

"Right." The doctor gave her a tight smile. "I'll see you in two weeks."

As soon as the door closed behind the doctor,

Shelby said, "Help me up."

"You just woke from a coma." He stepped up beside her. "Don't you think it's a little too soon for you to stand?"

"You heard the doctor. As soon as I can walk down the hall and back, I'm out of here." She gripped his arm with one hand and eased off the bed. When she landed on her feet, she realized for the first time that she was wearing ugly yellow hospital socks with skid-proof dots across the soles.

Fortunately, her legs held her weight, if a little shakily. But, by God, she'd make it to the end of the hall and back if it killed her.

"I hate hospitals," she muttered, leaning heavily on Remy.

"Yeah," he said. "Me, too. Come on. Let's get you there and back."

As they started for the door, Remy slipped an arm around her back and then stopped short. "Uh, you might want to rethink the hospital gown situation."

Heat filled Shelby's cheeks. With her free hand, she reached behind her to close the gap.

"Can you stand on your own for a second?" Remy asked.

Shelby nodded.

He let go of her, opened one of the cabinets in the room and pulled out a fresh hospital gown. He shook out the folds and held it out. "Wear it like a robe."

Shelby slid her arms into the gown and tied it in

the front, giving Remy a weak smile. "Thanks. I hate being a burden."

"You're not a burden."

"That's right. You're here to protect. It's your job." She started toward the door without his help. When her knees wobbled, he was there instantly, his arm wrapping around her waist.

"Everyone who knows you, knows you're a badass," he murmured. "You don't have to be strong all the time."

"If I want out of here, I sure as hell do." For all her bravado, she still leaned into him, angry at how weak she was from her ordeal.

"You'll be back to your old self before you know it," Remy said.

She glanced over at him, her brow furrowing. "Complete with memories?"

"You heard the doctor." He grinned. "Most likely. Count yourself lucky. Some brain injuries are so severe, the patient loses all memories and has to be taught the basics all over, like how to hold a spoon or tie her shoes."

"Okay," she snapped. "I get the picture. I wasn't lucky to be attacked, but I'm lucky my injuries aren't severe. Let's roll."

"Touchy." Remy pulled the door open and stepped out into the hall with Shelby.

She started out walking slowly, getting used to the skid-proof socks. As her muscles remembered how to work properly, she leaned less on Remy and stood straighter.

By the time they reached the end of the hall, she felt much better, to the point she didn't need Remy's arm around her anymore.

But she didn't ask him to remove it. She liked how strong and muscular it was and how it made her feel protected. Like a shield against a potential attacker.

She was still in shock over the fact that someone had tried to kill her in the bayou and in the hospital. Who would do such a thing?

As they closed in on their starting point and the end of her endurance run, a big man with broad shoulders and a fierce scowl emerged from her room.

Shelby stepped back into the curve of Remy's arm.

"It's okay," Remy said. "He's with me."

She frowned. "You didn't say anything about having a partner."

"Sorry, I didn't think you'd be awake so soon." He nodded toward the man. "Shelby Taylor, this is Gerard Guidry. He's also with the Brotherhood Protectors, and he's my backup on this mission. I texted him as soon as you started to wake."

Gerard held out his hand. "Deputy Taylor. It's good to see you up and about."

"Thank you." She smiled at Gerard and turned a cocked eyebrow on Remy. "Were there any other people besides the medical staff in my room while I was out?"

Remy's lips twisted. "One other. It took time for me and Gerard to fly down from Montana. We had a man named Tyson King stand guard over you until we could get here."

Shelby shook her head. "You two flew all the way from Montana?" Shelby narrowed her eyes. "What's a hometown boy from Bayou Mambaloa doing in Montana?"

He grinned. "Receiving my orientation into my new job as a Brotherhood Protector."

Shelby pinched the bridge of her nose. "I'll have to trust you on that. My head aches, and I need to sit before I fall."

"Right." Gerard pushed through the door into her room and held it open.

Remy slipped his arm around Shelby's back again and walked with her to the bed, where she sat on the edge.

"Do I have any clothes I can wear when I leave this place?" she asked. "Or will I have to wear these gowns out?"

"J.D. LaDue dropped off a bag your sister put together for you. It's in the closet." Remy crossed to the closet.

Inside were two plastic garbage bags. He lifted the one on top and peered inside. "These are your clean clothes and shoes." He handed them to her and looked into the other bag. "This must be what's left of your uniform." His nose wrinkled. "Yup. Smells like swamp water." He closed the bag and wrapped the drawstring around it several times. "I'm not sure what you can salvage from it, but we'll take it with us when we leave."

A knock sounded on the door.

"Come in," Shelby called out. "I hope it's the nurse with my discharge papers."

A nurse entered, carrying a sheaf of papers, followed by a man in dark slacks and a matching jacket with a New Orleans Police Department patch sewn on the front.

The nurse grimaced. "I'm here to go over your discharge, but first, Detective Saulnier would like to ask you some questions about the attack." She stepped to the side, allowing the detective through the door.

"Good morning, Miss Taylor." He held out his hand and gave hers a firm shake. "Or should I say Deputy Taylor?"

"You can call me Shelby," she said.

"Mr. Guidry was good enough to let me know you woke up this morning. I came as soon as I could." The detective flipped open a small notepad and pulled a pen from his pocket. "I also came in the night you were admitted after you were attacked in your hospital bed. From what I could get out of the staff, they were all responding to a code blue when you were attacked. No one saw the man come in, but a nurse saw one leave your room. Can you tell me anything about your attacker?"

Shelby gave a short, sharp laugh. "Nothing. Absolutely nothing. I just woke up less than an hour ago. I don't remember anything that happened to me for the past few weeks, much less the past two nights." She flung her hands in the air, tears filling her eyes. One slipped out and ran down her cheek. "Damn it." She brushed the tear aside. "Deputies don't fuckin' cry."

"I'm sorry this happened to you, Deputy—Shelby." The detective gave her a gentle smile. "I had to ask, just in case you came to before the man attacked."

Shelby drew a deep breath, gathered her crumbling reserves and lifted her chin. "I understand. I apologize for losing my shit. I'll be okay as soon as I get out of this hospital."

Saulnier nodded. "I hate hospitals." Saulnier pulled a card out of his pocket. "You know the drill."

"Yeah." Shelby smiled. "If I remember anything of use, I'll give you a call. Hell, if I remember anything, I'll turn backflips."

After the detective left, Shelby's gaze went to the nurse. "Let's do this. No offense, but I'm ready to get the hell out of here."

The nurse laughed and quickly went through the papers. When she was done, she asked, "Need help getting dressed?"

"Maybe." Shelby gave Remy a pointed glance. "If you two could step outside, I'll only be a minute."

Remy and Gerard exited.

"I'll stay to make sure you don't fall," the nurse said. "If you need help, just ask. Otherwise, you're on your own. I ordered a wheelchair to be brought up. It should be here soon."

"Thanks." Shelby dumped the bag of clothes on the bed, thankful her sister had the foresight to send them. She smiled. Chrissy was a good mother to her children. She'd been Shelby's second mom when their mother had to work full-time to support her two daughters after she'd divorced her husband. Sure, he'd paid child support, but the money had only gone so far.

Chrissy and Shelby didn't have much to do with their father. He'd cheated on their mother with his secretary. Their mother hadn't found out about it until his secretary had shown up on her doorstep with the news that she was pregnant.

Their mother hadn't screamed or cried. She'd packed their father's clothes and personal items, set them on the front porch, changed the locks and filed for divorce.

Their father had signed, no argument. Once the divorce was final, he'd married his secretary, and they'd moved from Bayou Mambaloa to Atlanta and hadn't looked back.

Which left the three women to fend for themselves. Chrissy had had her driver's license by then and had helped make sure Shelby wasn't forgotten.

As Shelby dressed in the clothes her sister had gone to her cottage to collect, she marveled at her sister. Once again, she'd come through. With five boys to wrangle, Chrissy had her hands full. But she always found a way to help Shelby.

Once Shelby was finished dressing, she thanked the nurse.

The nurse left, and a medical assistant entered with a wheelchair. "Hi, I'm Lindsay. I'll be escorting you to the exit."

Shelby frowned at the chair. "I can walk."

Lindsay gave her a nice smile. "Hospital rules. If you come in on a gurney, you leave in a wheelchair."

Shelby lowered herself into the chair and let the assistant wheel her out the door and down the hallway to the elevator.

Remy fell in step beside the chair. "Feel better in your own clothes?"

Shelby's lips twisted. "Almost normal, less several weeks of memory. Where's Gerard?"

"He's bringing the car to the pickup point," Remy said. "He'll drive us to Bayou Mambaloa."

"Good. I want to find out who did this to me."

"You heard the doctor. You can't go to work until he clears you."

"So, I'm not going back to work. But I can ask questions in an unofficial capacity. If that leads me to the people who tried to kill me, good. I have a huge bone to pick with them." She glanced up at Remy. "If you're going to be my protector until we catch these guys, you can do all the driving. But we're going to find those bastards if it's the last thing I do."

CHAPTER 6

REMY SETTLED Shelby in the back seat of the SUV, walked around to the passenger side and got in next to her. He brought up the map application on his phone and keyed in the address for the Broussard Country Store. Once he had the location, he shared it with Gerard's phone.

Gerard slid in behind the steering wheel, connected his phone to the SUV's computer and brought up the directions. By the time they hit the streets, the morning traffic had settled. They made it out of the city in good time.

Remy turned to Shelby. "I'm going to call Hank Patterson, the man behind Brotherhood Protectors. He's an ex-Navy SEAL with years of training and experience in tough situations. I want to bring him up to speed on what's happened since I got here and see if he has any information that can help us."

Shelby shrugged. "Why are you telling me this? He's *your* boss."

"Because I'm going to put the call on speaker so you can be a part of the conversation. Are you up to that?"

"Yes," she said with a frown puckering her brow. "I'm okay, just a little weak from lying in bed for two days. I can still hold my own."

Remy grinned and called headquarters.

Hank answered on the first ring. "Remy, tell me what you know."

Remy put the phone on speaker. "Shelby's awake. She's been released from the hospital, and we're on the way to Bayou Mambaloa. She's listening in on this conversation."

"Good morning, Miss Taylor," Hank said. "We're glad you're back with us. I have my tech guy, Swede, listening in as well."

"Glad you're feeling better," Swede seconded. "No lasting damage or major injuries?"

"Nothing I can't get over in my own home," Shelby said. "Thanks for asking."

"Were you able to tell the police who rammed your boat or tried to smother you?" Hank asked.

Remy glanced at Shelby. She waved her hand, urging him to answer. "No. She can't remember anything about either incident or anything that has happened for as far back as almost a month."

"Nothing," she confirmed, pinching the bridge of

her nose. "Not a damned thing."

"I spoke with Sheriff Bergeron," Hank said. "He accompanied J.D. LaDue and an investigator from the Louisiana Crime Investigation Division out to where J.D. found Shelby. Her boat was still there, but there was no sign of the craft that hit her. They're keeping an eye out for any watercraft that looks like it was used as a battering ram. They searched a wide area around the location for anything that might indicate illegal activity that Miss Taylor might've witnessed. Something severe enough that would make them want to hush any witnesses."

"And?" Remy prompted.

"The sheriff said Miss Taylor was looking for a drug cartel drop. She was supposed to note anything suspicious and get out."

"In other words, do not engage," Shelby said. "So, I was looking for a drug drop."

"Any of this jogging a memory?" Remy asked.

She shook her head. "No."

"They found some impressions in the moss on one of the islands," Hank said. "Someone had placed what appeared to be heavy boxes on the ground at some point. The moss was spongy, and most of the tracks had recovered by the time they got to that island. They might not have seen it if the moss hadn't been ripped up in some places."

"Sheriff Bergeron said Louisiana's CID is investigating the case and is in touch with the Drug Enforcement Agency to assist," Swede said.

"Great," Shelby said. "CID and DEA will muck around and get nowhere. They don't know the bayou like we do."

"The DEA has been following the Equis Cartel based out of Colombia, with connections in Miami, Atlanta and New York City," Swede said. "They've been leaning heavily on those locations over the past six months, spearheading several million-dollar busts. They think the cartel might have shifted their operations to New Orleans and surrounding areas."

"What better place to get lost in than the bayou?" Shelby said. "But they'd have to connect with locals to find their way around. Find their local connection, and you'll find the runners or drop locations."

"But that doesn't stop the supply chain completely," Hank said.

"No. It just plugs one hole," Swede said. "Another will spring up somewhere else. That's why the DEA wants in. They want to chase the chain all the way to Colombia and eliminate the source."

"Wow," Shelby said. "Someone in the DEA told you all that?"

"No," Swede said. "No one told me anything."

Remy's gaze met Shelby's. "Swede has special talents."

"Is mind reading one of them?" Shelby asked.

Hank chuckled. "He knows things."

Shelby frowned. "If what Swede's saying is accurate, and Equis is moving operations to New Orleans, the DEA should be all up in our business in Bayou Mambaloa."

"If Equis has set up shop in Bayou Mambaloa, you and the entire community could be in a whole lot of trouble," Hank said.

"The cartel is named after the Equis Snake, the deadliest snake in Colombia," Swede said. "Its venom is loaded with protein-degrading enzymes that can cause a variety of health issues, most notably necrosis. And they like to hang out where humans live."

"The snake is greatly feared by Colombians, as is the Equis Cartel," Hank said. "The cartel is known for being ruthless. Anyone who gets in their way is eliminated, sometimes in horrible ways to convince others not to cross them."

"Like ramming a boat and then trying to drown the person who was in it?" Remy asked, his stomach knotting.

"Quite possibly," Swede said. "And they didn't hesitate to make another attempt while she was in the hospital."

"If Equis is behind the attacks," Shelby said, "they won't leave me alone until I'm no longer a threat."

Remy reached for Shelby's hand. She let him take it and curled her fingers around his.

"That's why Gerard and Remy are there," Hank

said. "The rest of Remy's team is packing up. They'll head out in the morning."

Shelby's eyes rounded. "There are more of you coming?"

"Ten, counting me," Remy said. "I'm setting up a branch of Brotherhood Protectors in Bayou Mambaloa. We'll take on clients in Louisiana, Texas, Mississippi and anywhere we're needed in the south."

Shelby frowned. "Does Sheriff Bergeron know about this? I can tell you he won't be happy to have a bunch of vigilantes getting in the way of the law."

Hank chuckled. "I had that conversation with the sheriff. He said the same thing. I assured him we wouldn't get in his way. We're a protection, rescue and extraction service. The sheriff admitted his department is understaffed. The New Orleans Police Department can't keep up with the crime in and around the city. They don't have time or the manning to provide bodyguards for individuals who find themselves in difficult situations—like you, Miss Taylor."

"I don't need a bodyguard," she said. "I can take care of myself."

"In most situations, that's probably true," Hank said. "This isn't most situations. Equis Cartel has deep pockets and a long reach. If one member can't get the job done, they'll send more. You'll constantly be looking over your shoulder."

"You, by yourself, won't be enough," Remy said. "You need someone to have your back."

"Remy's right," Hank said. "Brotherhood Protectors understand the concept. They've had it drilled into their heads through specialized training in various branches of the military and experience with multiple deployments in hostile territory. I trust each of these men with my life and the lives of my wife and children. I wouldn't have invited them to join the team if I didn't have faith in their abilities, work ethic and teamwork."

"Sounds like there's going to be a lot of people converging on Bayou Mambaloa," Shelby said. "Won't Equis move to a less populated area?"

"From what I was able to find," Swede said, "they're going to infiltrate slowly so as not to draw attention. The DEA already has a couple of undercover agents in the community."

Shelby's eyes widened. "Really? Bayou Mambaloa is a small town. Everyone knows everyone else." Her eyes narrowed. "Except during tourist season when people come to the bayou to fish, go on airboat tours and enjoy the festivals and zydeco music."

"Right," Swede said. "A DEA agent might have come in as a retiree there for a summer of fishing."

"Or a photographer or painter, wanting to capture the beauty of the bayou," Shelby said softly. "As far as that goes, whatever drug cartel, if it's Equis, could have infiltrated in the same manner, and their contacts could be what we might consider to be legitimate fishing guides or airboat tour boat drivers."

"True," Hank said.

"We don't have concrete evidence on the Equis Cartel connection," Swede said. "We just know the DEA is interested in Bayou Mambaloa as a possible drop point for product passing through."

"Whoever is in the bayou, Equis or not," Remy said, "is dangerous."

"So, be on your guard at all times," Hank said. "Remy, you be looking for the rest of your team to arrive in three days or less."

"Roger," Remy said.

"Out here," Swede and Hank said in unison.

"Out here," Remy replied and ended the call.

He still held Shelby's hand in his. She hadn't pulled it free. "Are you okay?"

She shook her head. "I'm a deputy sheriff in a small town. Sure, we have our share of drug dealers and meth-heads and the occasional murder to investigate, but this—" She raised her head and met Remy's gaze.

Her brow dipped low. Worry etched lines across her forehead. "Bayou Mambaloa is my home. My family lives there. Chrissy, Alan and the boys…"

Remy gently squeezed her hand. "We don't know for certain that the Equis Cartel is behind the attack."

"No, but someone was. And they came after me in New Orleans. If I go back to Bayou Mambaloa, they'll follow me and try again." Her fingers tightened around his. "What if they come after me when I'm with my sister and her kids?" She shook her head. "I love those boys. I couldn't live with myself if something happened to them."

Remy glanced in the rearview mirror, catching Gerard's gaze.

Gerard nodded in silent agreement.

"We'll position Gerard with your sister and her family. If the DEA and the cartel can infiltrate Bayou Mambaloa undercover, so can we. The cartel doesn't have to know I'm your bodyguard and Gerard is your sister's."

Shelby's eyes narrowed. "Alan does need help at that store. It would be natural to hire an extra hand. Chrissy does what she can between chasing after the twins and caring for baby Marty."

Remy nodded. "That would be a perfect cover for him. Working at the store will keep him close to Chrissy and her family."

"What about you?" Shelby looked up into his eyes. "Getting you hired into the sheriff's department would be easy, but we'd be on different shifts."

"You're not going back to work for a couple of weeks," he reminded her.

Shelby frowned. "I feel better."

When Remy opened his mouth, Shelby held up her hand. "I know. I'd be a danger to the community.

But that's fine. I'll be free to investigate on the down low."

Remy shook his head. "Too obvious. You need a cover, and so do I."

"Remy can be your former boyfriend back in town looking to rekindle an old flame," Gerard said.

Remy and Shelby both looked at Gerard in the rearview mirror.

"That would work," Remy said with a grin. "Since you'll be on sick leave, you could show me around town. I need to find a building where I can set up our regional office. We also need to find lodging for my team."

Shelby's frown dipped deeper.

"I can't have your back twenty-four-seven if I'm not with you twenty-four-seven," Remy pointed out. "And since I'm just moving back to town, I don't have a place to stay…"

Her frown lifted. "Whether you're pretending to be an old flame or an old friend, it makes sense for you to stay with me while you're looking for a place of your own. I have a spare bedroom in my house." She drew in a deep breath and let it out. "I don't like that my town is potentially under siege by a Colombian drug cartel. This is America, not some third-world country. Things like this don't happen." She looked from Gerard's reflection back to Remy. "Do they?"

Remy's lips pressed together. He'd like to tell her

they didn't happen, but they did, more than most people would believe. "Let's hope we're wrong and we're overreacting."

Shelby shook her head. "I'd rather overreact and be prepared than do nothing. I won't stand by and let people I love die because I couldn't believe it would happen to us." She squared her shoulders. "I'll work with Chrissy and Alan to 'hire' Gerard. Since he's a friend of yours and new in town, they can put him up at their house."

Remy raised his eyebrows. "Your sister has five kids. Do they have room for a guest?"

"They live in the old Cranston House."

"We used to throw rocks through the windows of that house." Remy shook his head. "I thought they would have torn that place down years ago."

Shelby laughed. "In a shrewd business deal, Alan bought it for the money owed in back taxes. They've spent the last fifteen years restoring it a little at a time. Their latest room restoration was the bonus room over their garage. Gerard can stay there until he can find a place of his own. The bonus room has its own outside staircase entrance but is also accessible from the main part of the house, so he can keep an eye on the family."

Gerard nodded. "I'm okay with that as long as your sister and her family are in agreement."

Shelby frowned. "The only thing is that I'm not

sure my sister and her husband can pay you much. Certainly not what a bodyguard would make."

Gerard exchanged a smile with Remy. "They don't have to worry about that. Hank's philosophy is to help people whether they can pay or not."

Shelby cocked an eyebrow. "What kind of business does that? How can you make a living doing that?"

"Hank Patterson and his wife, Sadie McClain, have enough," Remy said. "And many of their clients who can afford the cost of a bodyguard pay extra to help others who can't."

Shelby's fingers tightened around Remy's. "Remind me to thank Hank and his wife."

"I will." Remy leaned back against the seat. With a plan in place, they'd have a shot at snooping around town and the bayou without being too obvious that they were looking for the local cartel connection and possible drug drop locations. All under the pretext of looking for a place to set up a business and a place to live. All the while, he'd be performing his number one mission...protecting Shelby.

He turned to the woman beside him.

She'd leaned her head back against the seat and closed her eyes.

For a long time, he studied her face, memorizing the curve of those lips he'd kissed so thoroughly and the way her dark lashes lay against her cheeks. She was beautiful. What he wouldn't give to kiss her now.

One of her eyelids rose. "You're staring at me."

"You really don't remember me?" he asked with a crooked smile.

Her other eye opened as well. "It's like that thought you were thinking a moment ago and now can't remember. It's there at the back of your mind, but it won't come forward. I know you. I just can't place you. How long were you away from Bayou Mambaloa?"

"Twenty years until almost a month ago. I came back on vacation after separating from the Navy."

"Do you look very different from when you lived here all those years ago?"

He chuckled. "A bit. I was a skinny teenager when I left."

Her gaze roamed over his broad shoulders. "That could be it." Her voice lowered, and her eyes flared. "You're not a skinny teenager anymore."

His groin tightened at the huskiness in her tone. She'd whispered naughty words into his ear in that same tone when they'd made love during the storm.

"Did we date back then?" she asked.

He laughed. "No. I was eighteen. You were a punk thirteen-year-old."

"You're my sister's age, then." Her eyes narrowed. "Did you two date?"

He nodded, tensing. "We did until she broke it off. I was headed into the military. She didn't want that kind of life." He shrugged. "I can't blame her. She would've been unhappy moving every two to four years and spending much of her time alone."

Shelby nodded. "Despite how chaotic her life is, she loves being the mother of five boys and helping Alan with the store. She loves Bayou Mambaloa and never wanted to leave, even after our mother moved to Charleston, South Carolina, with her new husband. Not me. I couldn't wait to leave this little town behind."

"And yet, you're back." He caught her gaze. "Why?"

"I moved to Memphis after I graduated college. Three years there made me realize it's not the place that holds you. It's the people. I had no one in Memphis, even after three years. Mom had her new husband and new life in Charleston. I missed my dearest and possibly my only friend...my sister." Shelby closed her eyes, a smile tilting her lips. "So, I came home to family."

She leaned up and turned a fierce frown on Remy. "And nobody better mess with the people I love, or I'll personally make sure they regret it to their dying day."

Remy fought back the smile that wanted to spread across his face at the fiery passion on Shelby's face. God, she was beautiful, even though her blond hair hadn't been brushed and she didn't have a bit of makeup on her face. Her surface beauty wasn't what attracted Remy to Shelby. He was attracted to her strength, bravery, loyalty to family and the unashamed and unfettered passion she brought to everything she did, including sex.

Chances were, she might never remember what they'd shared in the fishing hut. He couldn't bank on building something out of what was now a one-sided memory.

If he wanted another chance with Shelby, he had to start over, win her trust and then her heart.

For a man who wasn't afraid of charging into an enemy hot zone, Remy was scared. When they'd been together that first and only time, it had been a shared passion. Lust. It had been good for a one-night stand, but lust alone wasn't what long-lasting relationships were built on.

What if she'd recognized that then? What if she'd insisted on only that one night together because she'd felt the lust but nothing deeper?

He shot another glance in her direction. He might be afraid of fucking it up, but Remy Montagne wasn't a quitter. When he wanted something badly enough, he worked his ass off to get it. That's how he'd made it through Navy SEAL BUD/S training and twenty years of service.

Shelby Taylor might not remember a stormy night in the bayou, but Remy would be sure to give her new memories she'd cherish for the rest of her life. A life she'd share with him.

He just had to take care of one little thing first.

The matter of someone wanting to kill her.

A cartel with a hit out on his girl could put a damper on his plan to woo the determined deputy.

"Remy?" Shelby said softly, her eyes closed and her lips parted ever so slightly.

"Yes?" he answered, wondering if she had even the slightest clue about what was going through his mind.

"When we get to Bayou Mambaloa, I want to go to the location where J.D. found me."

"Shouldn't you rest for a day or two before we dive into the investigation?"

"The longer we wait, the harder it will be to find any evidence that CID might have missed."

"If you think you're up to it, we'll go."

"You sure that's a good idea?" Gerard asked.

Remy snorted. "I know it's a bad idea, but if I don't take her, she'll go without me." He met Shelby's gaze. "Am I right?"

"Damn right." She gave him a challenging smile. "The doctor said I couldn't drive a car. He didn't say anything about driving a boat."

Gerard laughed. "I think five little boys might be a lot easier to handle than one deputy sheriff on medical leave."

Shelby grinned. "You say that now. Don't get me wrong. I love all five of my nephews, but there is nothing easy about wrangling them. My sister is a saint and a magician."

As Gerard drove into the small town of Bayou Mambaloa, he slowed. "Which way?"

"To the marina," Shelby answered promptly and gave him the directions.

"You can drop us off and head for Broussard Country Store. It's on the corner of the town square," Shelby said. "You can't miss it. I'll call my sister and let her know what's going on so that you don't blindside her and her husband. Alan can be a little jealous at times."

A frown dented Gerard's forehead. "He's not one of those guys who shoots first and asks questions later?"

"Not at all," Shelby said with a grin. "But he's very possessive of my sister."

"Duly noted. I'll keep my hands, eyes and thoughts about her to myself," Gerard said. "Besides, she's not my type."

"How do you know?" Shelby asked.

"She's married," Gerard answered promptly. "I won't mess with another man's woman."

"Good," Shelby said. "Now, turn here. The marina is at the end of this road."

Gerard stopped in the marina parking lot.

Shelby pointed toward an older pickup parked in the shade of an oak tree. "That's my truck, parked in my usual spot."

"Do we need to go through the bag with your ruined uniform to find the keys?" Remy asked.

Shelby shook her head. "No, I leave the keys in the truck."

When Remy frowned, Shelby said, "What? I can't take them out on the bayou. What if I lost the keys in the water? Do you know how hard it would be to find them?"

"Good point." Remy pushed open his door and stepped out.

He offered his hand to Shelby.

She let him help her out of the vehicle and leaned against the fender.

Remy strode to the back of the rental car, opened the hatch and located his handgun and shoulder holster. Sliding the straps over his arms, he secured the buckle in front and slid his gun into the holster. Then he dug a light jacket out of his duffel bag. Despite the heat and humidity, he pulled the windbreaker over his shoulders, hiding the holster beneath.

Gerard appeared beside him. "Hank loaded a couple of bulletproof vests in the gym bag with the communications equipment."

Remy reached into the bag, pulled out one of the vests and handed it to Shelby.

She didn't argue. Instead, she put it on and secured the buckles. She patted the vest, looking around a little lost.

"What's wrong?" Remy asked.

Her lips twisted in a wry grin. "I feel out of uniform."

"You're not in uniform," he said.

"I know, but the vest makes me feel like I should be in uniform. And I don't have my gun. I wonder if it went down with the boat?" Her brow furrowed. "Speaking of which...there's a lot of paperwork involved with losing your service weapon. When we get back from the bayou, I should stop by the station and get on that report."

"And what would you put in your report?"

She blinked several times. "I guess only two words. I forgot." She shook her head. "Gerard, you do have the best assignment. My sister is sweet. The boys will love you, and none of them are as over-the-top crazy as their Auntie Shelby. On the other hand, Remy will be challenged by me." She repeated the directions to the store.

Shelby turned to Remy. "Ready?"

Remy hefted his rifle in one hand and took Shelby's hand with his free one. "I should be asking you that question. I'm not the one who got knocked in the head, nearly drowned, and then almost suffocated."

"I'm fine," she insisted.

"Well, I'm not," he said. "But let's get going."

And hope we don't run into an army of cartel hitmen along the way.

CHAPTER 7

"Oh, Shelby, honey!" Chrissy cried. "I'm so glad you're okay. I was so worried."

Shelby held Remy's cell phone away from her ear as her sister gushed her relief. When she quieted, Shelby settled the phone against her ear. "I'm already back in Bayou Mambaloa," she said.

"Why didn't you call me before you left the hospital? I would've met you at your house with a pot of chicken gumbo."

Shelby smiled. Her sister's cure-all for anything that ailed you was a pot of chicken gumbo. Not plain old chicken soup. No, it had to be gumbo. "I got a bump on my head, not the flu," Shelby protested. "Besides, I'm not at my place yet. I won't be there for an hour or more."

"I would've thought you'd go home and straight to bed," Chrissy's mind-your-mother voice came through the receiver into Shelby's ear. "Surely, the doctor told you to take it easy."

"He did tell me I couldn't go back to work until he cleared me. I have a follow-up visit with him in two weeks."

"Well, at least you won't have to go back to work yet. I wish you didn't work for the sheriff's department. None of this would've happened if you'd chosen another career field."

Shelby sighed. Chrissy had never wanted Shelby to go into law enforcement. She'd hoped that when Shelby went off to college, she'd pursue a career in nursing or accounting.

Shelby had gotten her degree in forensics, much to Chrissy's disappointment. Then she'd gone to work in Memphis, one of the most dangerous cities in the South and nowhere close to home.

Shelby might have stayed in Memphis if things had worked out differently. After paying her dues as a street cop, she'd been passed over twice for promotion to detective. The positions had gone to guys with less experience on the force and less formal education.

What they'd had were testicles and connections in the good-old-boy system. When the guy she'd been dating at the time got one of those positions, when he'd sworn he hadn't applied and wasn't interested, Shelby had had enough. She'd turned in her two weeks' notice and headed back to Bayou Mambaloa.

At least working for the sheriff's department, she had to be a jack of all trades. She'd have her shot at investigation and picking through clues. Bayou Mambaloa was too small to be able to afford its own police force. The parish sheriff's department had to handle all law enforcement issues.

"Is Remy still with you?" Chrissy asked.

Shelby shot a glance toward Remy as he negotiated the boat rental with Mitch Marceau, the owner of the marina. "Yes, I'm still with Remy."

"You weren't mad at me for calling him?" Chrissy asked.

Shelby frowned. "Mad? Why would I be mad?"

"I don't know. You got all moody after he left town following his last visit. I thought maybe something happened between the two of you."

"I'm having memory issues from the bump on my head," Shelby admitted. "Did something happen between me and Remy?"

"You don't remember?" Chrissy asked.

"No." Shelby stared at the man being discussed. "When was he last in town?"

"He didn't mention it?"

Chrissy answering questions with questions was beginning to annoy Shelby. "No, he didn't mention that he was in town recently. He only said he hadn't lived in Bayou Mambaloa for twenty years."

"He served in the Navy all those years as a Navy SEAL. I'm surprised you don't remember that,"

Chrissy said. "You must have hit your head pretty hard. You cried when he left, even though he'd been *my* boyfriend."

"I never cry," Shelby muttered.

Chrissy chuckled. "That's what was so disturbing. You cried so hard you made yourself sick. Even my gumbo wouldn't console you."

A vague memory swam through the fog in her head. She was crying, and Chrissy was holding her, telling her he'd be back someday.

"That was Remy?" Shelby asked.

"Yes, it was."

"I remember the names of everyone who lives in town, but for the life of me, I don't remember his." Shelby continued to stare at the man, wondering why her brain had blocked her memories of Remy.

"That's so weird," Chrissy said. "But don't worry, I'm sure you'll get those memories back. Give your head time to recover. Did the police catch the guy who tried to smother you in the hospital?"

"No." Shelby noticed Remy and Mitch shaking hands. Remy turned to Shelby and waved for her to join him. "I have to go now. I'll touch bases with you as soon as I know anything."

"Will Remy be staying with you until they figure out who attacked you in the bayou?"

"Yes."

"Sleeping in your house?" her sister persisted.

Heat burned in Shelby's cheeks. "In the spare bedroom."

"Uh-huh," her sister said with her mama-can-see-right-through-you tone. "Just remember to use protection."

"It's not like that," Shelby insisted. "He's only there to have my back until we find out who's behind all this bullshit."

"Oh, sweetie. I'm so sorry this is happening. You should come stay with us."

"No," Shelby was quick to say. "I'm staying as far from you, Alan and the kids as possible. I don't want any of you to be collateral damage if they make another attempt on my life."

"You think they'll try again?" Chrissy asked.

"Yeah." She drew in a breath. "That's why Remy is sending over one of his guys to hang out with your family. He'll be your protection until we don't need it anymore."

"Wow. You're scaring me even more than I was scared for you," Chrissy said softly. A baby cried in the background. "Shh, Marty. I'll be there in just a minute," she called out.

"Thing is, we don't want people to think we're hiring bodyguards," Shelby said. "Gerard Guidry is headed your way as we speak. Have Alan fake-hire him to help in the store. It gives him a valid reason to be with your family. And he's new in town, so he'll need a place to stay.'

"The newly renovated bonus room would work, don't you think?" Chrissy offered.

Shelby grinned. "That would be perfect. That way, it looks like he has his own digs from the outside, but he'll also have access to the house should you need his help."

"Boy, you'd think small towns were safer than the city," her sister said. "Right now, I'm not so sure."

"Gerard, like the rest of the guys who work with Remy and his boss, are highly trained, special operations types. He'll take good care of you."

"Makes me feel marginally better," Chriss said. "And for the record, Remy and I never slept together. We dated, but I didn't sleep with him."

"Did *you* break up with him?" Shelby asked.

Chrissy chuckled. "I did. I think he was surprised. He was usually the one who broke up with the girls. But we parted friends. He wanted excitement and adventure. To see the world and get the hell out of Bayou Mambaloa. I wanted a home, stability, a husband who came home every night and, of course, children." She laughed. "I got everything I dreamed of, and I wouldn't trade it for anything."

"Until we get a handle on this situation, be super aware of strangers," Shelby warned.

"I will. And you be careful," Chrissy said. "You're the only sister I have and my best friend. I almost lost you once. Don't let that happen again."

Shelby grinned. "Yes, ma'am." She ended the call

and joined Remy on the jetty where he stood beside a small aluminum boat with a thirty-horsepower outboard motor attached to the back, chugging in the water, coughing out puffs of smoke every so often.

Shelby cocked an eyebrow. "That's all Mitch had?"

"We're in the middle of tourist season. All his fishing boats with more powerful motors have been rented out."

Shelby pressed her lips together. "Let's just hope we don't need to make a quick getaway. There won't be anything quick about that boat."

"I asked him to hold a more powerful boat for us tomorrow," Remy said. "We could wait until then to head out into the bayou."

Shelby shook her head. "I need to see where this all went down."

Remy dropped down into the boat and balanced while it rocked with his weight. When it steadied, he held out his hand to her.

She placed her hand in his and let him help her into the boat. "I'll drive." When he didn't move, she frowned. "The doctor didn't want me to drive a car. I can manage a boat. Besides, it's been years since you navigated the bayou. I'd prefer we didn't get lost."

"You've got the helm, Captain," he said with a grin and cupped her elbow, guiding her onto the bench near the handle on the motor. "I'll ride point and keep my eyes open for any possible bad guys lurking about." He settled on the bench in front of Shelby and half-turned to look back at her. "Do you know where you're going?"

Shelby frowned. "No. I guess I didn't think this through. I need to talk with J.D. He was the one who found me."

Remy grinned. "I spoke with Mitch. He said J.D. came by earlier to get gas for his boat. He told Mitch he found you just past his fishing hut. Do you remember where that is?"

Shelby closed her eyes and thought hard. "I know the bayou. My father took me fishing almost every weekend until he and Mom divorced." She opened her eyes. "Why can't I picture where J.D.'s fishing hut is?"

"It's okay. I know where it is."

Her eyes widened. "You do? After twenty years?"

Remy nodded, his gaze holding hers. "I've been there recently." He looked like he wanted to say more. Instead, he gave her a chin lift. "Drive. I'll tell you when and where you need to turn. And relax. Don't try to force your memories to return. It's possible you'll navigate the bayou on muscle memory." He leaned forward and untied the line holding the boat flush against the jetty.

Shelby drew in a deep breath, let it out slowly, and then maneuvered the little boat away from the marina and out into the bayou.

She'd never admit it out loud, especially to Remy, that her heart was beating too fast and her hands were slick with sweat. Her memory of what had happened to her was locked securely behind an impenetrable wall in her mind. Even though she couldn't remember what had happened, it didn't stop her from having a panic attack as she drove the boat into the bayou, where she'd almost lost her life two days before.

Following Remy's directions, she steered the little craft through the maze of islands, tributaries and inlets. For the most part, boating through the bayou was as natural to her as breathing. Like Remy said, she knew which ways to turn before he spoke.

When they rounded a large stand of cypress trees with branches hanging low over the water, a weathered hut came into Shelby's view. She eased back on the throttle and let the boat drift toward the building.

The ghost of a memory flitted through her mind. "I know this hut," she said. "I must have passed it a thousand times since I've roamed the bayou." Her eyes narrowed. "I think J.D. rents it out to people who want to escape to the bayou and just fish."

Remy turned to look at her. "Do you remember ever going inside the hut?"

She thought hard. "If I have, I can't picture it. I don't know. It's weird what I remember and what I can't. It's so random what my brain chooses to block out."

The little boat drifted up to the little dock extending out from the hut's front porch.

"We should look inside," Remy said. "Rule it out as a drug drop location." He tossed a line over a post and secured the boat to the dock.

"We don't have J.D.'s permission or a warrant to search," Shelby pointed out.

"You're not on duty."

"No, but I'm still required to follow the law," she said.

"Fine." Remy stepped up onto the dock. "I'll check it out."

CHAPTER 8

SHELBY'S TRAINING as an officer of the law told her that entering the hut without permission from the owner was not legal and could get her in big trouble. J.D. LaDue could take her to court or sue the sheriff's department.

Still, something about the place called to her. Was it a memory that had been locked behind the wall in her mind? If she went inside, would it trigger that memory to return?

What if that recollection had something to do with who'd attacked her?

"I'll come as far as the front door," Shelby said. "Someone has to have your back."

He chuckled. "How are you going to have my back when you don't even have a gun?"

She frowned. "I need to fix that. I have my personal handgun in a gun safe in my house. I'll get it out as soon as I get home and start carrying it. For now, though, at least I can warn you if someone comes up on you from behind."

"True. My lookout." He reached for her hand, gripped it tightly and pulled her up onto the dock.

She leaned into him until she got her balance, still a little shaky. Shelby hated being weak.

As a law enforcement female, she'd worked hard to be in top physical condition. Her training in the police academy had given her some self-defense skills, which she'd built on and improved by taking additional self-defense classes. She liked to think she could hold her own against a male attacker, even one who was stronger and outweighed her by a hundred pounds.

Unfortunately, she hadn't been able to defend herself when she'd been in a coma. She studied the man in front of her, admitting, if only to herself, that she was glad he'd come all the way from Montana to protect her.

Remy eased up to the window, his hand slipping beneath his jacket to the handgun tucked in the holster. He glanced through the dirty glass into the hut. "It's too dark inside to see anything from out here." He wrapped his hand around the doorknob and turned it.

The door opened inward.

"Apparently, J.D. doesn't lock his fishing hut," Shelby said.

"It's not breaking and entering if the door is unlocked, is it?" Remy said with a wink.

"You're walking a very gray line," Shelby said.

"I won't tell anyone if you won't." Remy stepped through the door, disappearing into the dark interior of the tiny hut.

He appeared in the doorway. "Are you coming in?"

"Against my better judgment," she muttered and stepped past him. For a long moment, she stood just inside the door, allowing her vision to adjust to the limited light making it through the dingy window.

"Now that you're inside, does anything look familiar?" Remy spoke softly. He stood so close she could feel the warmth of his breath stirring the hair by her temple.

A shiver of awareness skimmed across her skin. She moved deeper into the hut. Away from Remy and the way he made her body tingle.

She stood in the middle of the one-room shack, turning slowly, her gaze taking in the tiny table, a chair, a bed in the corner, and the thin mattress folded in half. A shadowy image faded in and out of her memory so quickly, it didn't take form and reveal itself. "I feel like, maybe, I might have been here." She stopped turning when she faced Remy, a frown pulling at her forehead. "It's like little ghosts teasing me with fleeting manifestations. Then they're gone."

Remy met her gaze, his eyes narrowed, jaw tight. "What kind of manifestation?"

"Nothing solid. Just movement."

Remy's blue eyes flared. "Movement like another person in the hut with you?"

She shrugged. "Maybe. Again, nothing I could define." Once more, her gaze swept the small room. "I don't see any evidence that this hut has been used as a drug trafficking drop."

"Agreed." Remy gave the hut one last glance and sighed. "It's basic and unrefined, but I can see its charm. And for all its weathered wood, it's sturdy. I bet it holds up well in a storm." He shot a glance toward her.

Shelby nodded. "It must hold up well. It looks like it's been here for a long time."

Again, Remy sighed. "Ready?"

Shelby nodded though she wasn't sure just how ready she was to see the place she'd almost been killed. Would she have a visceral reaction to seeing her boat lying upside down in the water?

The only way to find out was to face the inevitable and get it over with. The longer they took to get there, the more wound up she'd be. The anticipation was terrible.

Remy stepped to the side to allow her to pass.

Her shoulder brushed against him, sending a jolt of electricity through her. At that moment, another ghost of a memory flitted through her mind. Not so much like a picture. More like a feeling, as if being held in someone's arms. She stopped moving, closed her eyes and waited, hoping for more.

But as quickly as it had surfaced, it dove back behind the wall in her mind.

Remy touched her arm, his fingers against her skin, sending heat throughout her body. The sensation was a combination of confusion and arousal. Confusion because she couldn't bring back whatever memory it inspired, and arousal because…well, because he was a sexy man any woman would love to…touch…and be touched by.

If only she could remember him.

"Are you okay?" Remy asked.

"Yeah," she said and pushed past him before her knees buckled, and she collapsed in his arms. Now, there was a thought…

Remy helped her back into the boat. "Let me take it the rest of the way," he said.

Shelby sank onto the bench in front of Remy, her fingers curling around the lip of the metal as Remy guided the boat past the fishing hut, moving deeper into the bayou, skirting around several small islands and a field of marsh grass.

Shelby's breath lodged in her throat, and her pulse quickened as she stared across the field. Her eyes saw one view of the grass, her mind saw another. Instead of viewing it from a distance, she was in it, pushing through stalks so thick, she could barely move through them. Scarcely able to breathe. Fear choking her lungs as effectively as drowning in the murky bayou.

Shelby drew into herself, wrapping her arms around her middle as they rounded a bend in the marsh.

"Damn," Remy swore softly and eased off the throttle.

The boat continued forward, drifting toward what appeared to be a shiny aluminum sliver of a hump in the water, pushed up against the marsh grass.

"J.D. found me on that?" Shelby's heart fluttered, for a moment, unable to establish a steady beat. She pressed a hand to her chest, her breath lodged in her throat.

"That's what he said," Remy spoke softly.

As their boat drifted closer, Remy reached for the paddle and stuck it into the water, slowing their forward momentum. When they floated alongside the overturned aluminum boat, he whistled. "I can understand why your brain doesn't want you to remember."

The hull had large scrape marks on the side closest to them, the other side rested on smashed marsh grass.

Shelby stared at the damaged boat, the ravaged marsh grass and shivered. "How am I even here?" she whispered.

"None of it's coming back to you?" Remy asked.

"No. Just a feeling of..." she shook her head from side to side, "...horrible dread."

For a long moment, she stared at the boat, a dark cloud hovering in her mind, guarding her memory of what had happened here. Another shiver racked her body. Only this one didn't stop. She shook so hard her teeth clattered together.

"Hey," Remy said.

Shelby dragged her gaze from the ruined boat and turned to look back at Remy.

He held out his hand. "Come here."

She took his hand and let him guide her across the boat to settle on the seat beside him.

Remy wrapped his arm around her shoulders, pulled her body up against his and held her until the shivers ran their course.

She leaned against him, exhausted and disheartened.

"Why would someone do this?" she said.

"You had to have witnessed something, or someone, they didn't want you to see."

"They really didn't want me to make it out, did they?" she said, her voice small in the vastness of the bayou.

His arm tightened around her. "But you did. Which confirms the level of badass you are." He touched a finger beneath her chin and tipped her face up. "I'm glad you're a badass. The world would be a sadder place without you in it." He brushed his lips across her forehead. The warmth of his lips helped to dispel the chill inside her.

Shelby stared up into his eyes, her head tilting backward even more.

Remy bent to touch his mouth to hers. Softly at first.

Shelby curled her hand behind his neck and brought him closer, the movement so natural, she felt like she'd done it before.

The kiss deepened, his mouth claiming hers, his tongue pushing past her teeth to tangle and caress.

Shelby moaned, clinging to him like a life preserver in a swollen river, afraid to let go. Fearful that, if she did, the river would take her down like the bayou almost had.

When at last Remy raised his head, he met her gaze, a frown forming on his forehead. "Hey. It's going to be okay." His thumb brushed a tear from her cheek.

"Damn," she said. "Deputies don't cry."

"You nearly died. You're allowed."

"That doesn't bother me as much as losing my memory." She stared up into his eyes. "I know you. Don't I?"

His lips quirked on the corners. "Do you?"

Her brow puckered. "Don't do that."

"What?"

"Don't be vague. Either I know you, or I don't."

"I grew up in Bayou Mamba—"

She laid a hand on his chest. "Yeah, you said that before. It's a small town. We would've run into each other, but that's not what I mean." She shook her head, suddenly dizzy. She leaned her forehead against his chest. "I know that kiss," she murmured. "Like you said about knowing the bayou…muscle memory."

His chest shook beneath her fingertips, a chuckle rumbling from within. "Muscle memory, huh?" He tipped her chin up. "When your mind is ready, you'll remember what you need to know. And if you don't, you can fill your thoughts with new memories." He pressed a kiss to her forehead. "Right now, we need to get you home. It was too soon to bring you here."

Shelby shook her head carefully. "No. I had to see it. I hoped it would jog my memory. Apparently, I need those memories back in order to take down the bastards who tried to kill me."

"Your body and head have suffered significant trauma. Give them a chance to heal."

"They might try again before I have time to recover. I might not be so lucky the next time."

"You have me," he said. "I have your back. I won't let them hurt you." He cupped her cheek. "In the meantime, you need rest."

She frowned, wanting to argue that she couldn't rest as long as bad guys were out there, waiting for a chance to strike again.

But she just didn't have the strength.

Remy turned to the motor, grabbed the handle and gave the engine enough fuel to set the little boat in motion.

Slowly turning the craft, he headed back the way they came.

Shelby leaned against Remy, glad he was there.

She didn't like depending on anyone but wasn't foolish enough to believe she could fight off a swarm of Colombian drug traffickers, even at her best physical health. The way she felt now, she couldn't even defend herself against one.

She'd go home, go to bed and hope for a full recovery by morning. Tomorrow, she'd start her investigation with a vengeance. People couldn't try to kill her and think they'd get away with it. She'd find whoever was responsible and make them pay.

CHAPTER 9

THE TRIP back to the marina passed in silence, with Remy driving the boat, his gaze panning every inlet as he looked ahead for any signs of danger.

Like Shelby, Remy had hoped seeing the site where she'd been found and the surrounding area would trigger her memory.

In the hut, he could've sworn she'd had a flash of something that should have reminded her of the night they'd spent there during a helluva storm.

Alas, though the location had sparked something inside her, it wasn't enough to clear her head and let those memories flow freely.

Two boats passed them. Each time one came into view, Shelby tensed beside him and leaned closer.

Remy kept his grip on the motor handle light in case he needed to let go and reach for the gun in the holster beneath his jacket. He steered wide of the oncoming vessels. With both passings, nothing happened. The boats appeared to be charter fishing boats with tourists on board, ready to catch fish.

When they reached the marina, Remy cut the engine, tied the boat to the jetty and stepped out first.

He reached down, gripped Shelby's hand and pulled her up onto the dock. Though both feet made it to the wooden planks, her legs buckled, and she landed hard against his chest.

Remy caught and held her until she was steady on her feet. Even then, he didn't lower his arms. He leaned back and stared down into her eyes. "Are you going to make it?"

Shelby nodded. "Just a little unsteady. Thanks."

He grinned and lowered his arms. When he was sure she could stand on her own, he positioned himself beside her with a hand at the small of her back. "I just need to let Mitch know the boat is back, and then we can be on our way to your place."

She nodded and walked with him to the marina building.

When they stepped inside, it took a few seconds for Remy's eyes to adjust to the dim interior.

Several people moved about the store, selecting items from the shelves. Two men stood at the counter paying for a live bait. One of the two men was J.D. LaDue.

Behind the counter, Mitch nodded toward Remy and Shelby as they entered and crossed the room.

J.D. turned and dipped his head. "Deputy Taylor, good to see you standing on your feet."

Shelby gave the grizzled fisherman a twisted smile. "Thank you for pulling me out of the bayou. I probably wouldn't be here now if not for you."

J.D. shrugged. "Someone woulda come along."

"It could have been some of the people who left me there or an alligator looking for an easy meal." Shelby wrapped her arms around the older man's neck. "Thank you, J.D."

Remy almost laughed at how red the fisherman's face turned.

When Shelby let go and backed away, she glanced toward Mitch and the other man standing with J.D. "You're in the presence of a real-life hero. Mr. LaDue saved my life."

"Way to go, J.D." Mitch clapped him on the back. "Need more heroes like you around here."

J.D. ducked his head, his face burning a bright red. "Oh shucks, Miss Taylor. I ain't no such thing. Just being neighborly. We got to look out for each other in the bayou."

Shelby touched his arm. "You're a good neighbor, Mr. LaDue."

"J.D., ma'am. Mr. LaDue was my daddy. He's been gone now for a decade."

"And I'm Shelby," she said. "Since you saved my life, I expect we're close enough to be on a first-name basis. Besides, you've known me all my life."

J.D. grinned. "That I have. I've known you since you were that little tow-headed girl in pigtails, goin' fishin' with yer daddy every Saturday. Shame yer daddy left ya'll. But I'm glad you're with us still."

"Me, too." Once again, she hugged the old man, much to his red-faced embarrassment.

When she let go, he glanced at Remy standing behind her.

"Good to see you back, Remy," J.D. said. "You need to rent the fishin' hut again?"

Remy shook his head, fully aware of Shelby turning to face him with a frown pulling her eyebrows low. "No, thank you, J.D. I've made alternative arrangements with electricity and a flushing toilet."

"Anytime you wanna use the hut, you let me know," J.D. said. "Not many folks are up to roughin' it. Probably won't be a storm like the last time you were there."

"Thanks," Remy said. "I'll keep that in mind."

"J.D.," Shelby turned back to the old man. "Do you know anyone in the bayou who might be looking for extra cash and isn't too picky about what they have to do for it?"

J.D. blinked. "Why? You got someone you wanna lose in the bayou? Maybe the folks who left you there to die?"

Remy chuckled. "You want the job?"

J.D. nodded. "Don't like it when someone messes

with the good ones. The deputy is one of the good ones. Which I'm bettin' you already know."

Remy nodded. "Yes, sir. She's one of the good guys."

"You take good care of her." J.D. actually shook a finger at Remy. "I don't wanna find her face down in the bayou again."

"I'll do my very best," Remy said. "I'd like her to stick around a lot longer now that I'm back in town."

"You stayin'?" J.D. asked.

Remy nodded. "Shelby's putting me up at her place. While she's on medical leave, she's going to help me find a place for my business office."

"Good. Ain't safe around here. Not with strangers sneaking around the bayou." J.D. turned to Shelby. "You want me to go after those no-accounts? Make them alligator bait?"

"No. I'll go through the legal channels to take them down," Shelby said. "Though if you know anyone who might help me find them, I'd appreciate any information you can come up with or a name of someone who might know. Like you said, the bayou's not safe with people like that roaming around." She paused. "We think maybe the folks who tried to kill me could be running drugs. That's hard to do if you don't know your way around."

J.D. nodded. "I still get lost when I'm not payin' attention."

"Know anyone down on his luck, who might have

gotten sucked into drug running to earn a buck?" Shelby asked.

J.D.'s eyes narrowed. "Not right off the top of my head. But I'll keep my ears open and let you know if I hear anything of use."

"Same," Mitch said. "Can't have people afraid to go out in the bayou. It's bad for business."

Shelby smiled at the men. "Thank you. Anything, big or small, could help. Don't hesitate to call me or Sheriff Bergeron."

"I'd rather call you, Miss Taylor—Shelby," J.D. said, his cheeks reddening again. "You're better lookin' than the sheriff."

Remy laughed. "I haven't met the sheriff, but I'm sure you're right."

Shelby's cheeks turned a bright pink, and she touched a hand to her hair. "I don't know. I feel like something the cat dragged in. Probably smell like it, too."

"No, ma'am," J.D. said. "You smell just fine to me and look even better."

She patted his shoulder. "You're too kind, J.D. I'm headed to the house, a shower and night's sleep in my own bed, not what they call a bed in the hospital. Again, thank you for pulling me out of the bayou. I owe you."

"You don't owe me nothin', Miss Shelby," J.D. insisted.

Shelby glanced up at Remy. "Ready?"

REMY

He nodded, concerned over how pale she'd become. "Let's go." He hooked her arm and led her out of the store and up to where her truck was parked in the shade of a magnolia tree.

"The key's in the driver's side wheel well, stuck on a magnet." She leaned her back against the old truck and closed her eyes.

Remy ran his fingers around the wheel well until he found the key, like she said, stuck on a magnet. He plucked it free and straightened. "How old is this truck? I think my grandfather had this same model."

"It's an antique," Shelby said. "Sold new in 1967 with only fifty-two-thousand miles on it. I bought it off Charlie Hughes when he finally traded it in for one with an air-conditioner."

"So, this one doesn't have an air-conditioner?"

"No," she said and grinned. "But the engine runs great. It's easy to fix when something breaks, and I don't go far in it. Now, I'd die of heat stroke if my service vehicle didn't have a working AC unit."

Remy walked around the truck, looked under the chassis and checked beneath the hood for any signs of tampering or explosives. As he slid the key into the door and twisted, he made a note to himself to have Hank get his truck to him ASAP. "I don't think I've used a key to open a vehicle door in a decade. You really should consider upgrading to a model manufactured in this century."

"Have a little respect. I can do most of the work

on it myself." She cocked an eyebrow. "Do you own a truck?"

Remy nodded and opened the door. "Yeah. It's five years old, not sixty."

She crossed her arms over her chest. "Ever had to work on it?"

He shrugged. "No."

"Not even to change the oil?" she persisted.

Remy shook his head. "I have someone else do it."

Shelby snorted. "I can change my oil, swap out spark plugs and replace an alternator without paying a fortune for someone else to do it."

"Why would you?"

"I don't know what Navy SEAL retirement pay is, but sheriff's deputies aren't rolling in the dough. If my mother hadn't let me take over the payments on her cottage, I wouldn't have a place to live. Hell, I'd be living with my sister and her brood."

Before Remy could anticipate her move, Shelby pushed away from the fender and walked around to the passenger door. "Come on, Remy. I'm hungry and too tired to continue the investigation today. I need a good night's sleep without being poked and prodded by well-intentioned nurses and lab techs." She pulled herself up into the passenger seat and leaned her head back, closing her eyes.

Remy climbed into the driver's seat. "Do you have any food in your refrigerator?"

Shelby groaned. "A jar of pickles and half a hamburger I bought a week ago."

"If you can hold out a little longer, I'll stop at your sister's store for something to eat."

"I don't need to eat," she said. "I'm too tired."

"You might not need to eat, but I do." And he'd also make sure she had something to fill her belly. She wouldn't recover quickly if she didn't give her body the fuel it needed to mend itself.

"Whatever," she muttered. "I just know my sister. She'll want to talk. I'm too tired to talk. Besides, I spoke to her while you were renting the boat."

He inserted the key into the ignition and turned it. The engine turned over immediately.

"See?" Shelby's eyes were closed, but a smile tilted her lips. "Starts like a charm. I put a new starter in it a month ago."

Remy chuckled. "Is there anything you can't do? My masculinity is suffering here."

She snorted. "I always promised myself I would never *need* a man in my life. After my father chose his secretary over his wife and daughters, I watched my mother struggle to support us. She'd relied on my father's income for so long she had no marketable skills. She worked in the high school lunchroom during the day and waitressed at a bar at night on the weekends."

"Why did I not know this? I went to the high school."

"She didn't want to embarrass Chrissy, so she stayed in the back. She never came out when the students were present. It's ironic that she made more money in tips working two nights than she did all day in the lunchroom. And it took every bit of it to pay the mortgage, utilities and put food on the table. Chrissy looked after me while Mom worked."

Remy shook his head as he pulled out of the marina parking lot and drove up to Main Street. "Is that why you tagged along on our dates?"

Shelby nodded. "I thought I was old enough to stay home alone, but Chrissy felt responsible and insisted I come along."

Remy grinned. "You remember?"

Shelby's eyes widened. "Holy cow. I remember. You drove a Mustang convertible you rebuilt with your father. The engine ran fine, but the leather seats were so torn up, you had blankets over them."

Remy had almost forgotten that old Mustang. He'd spent the summer before his sixteenth birthday working with his father, rebuilding the engine. He'd worked in Charlie Hughes's fields, weeding, hoeing and picking produce to sell to the local stores and at the farmer's market to make enough money to buy parts for his car.

"You were so proud of that car," Shelby said softly.

Yes. He had been. "It was a labor of love between me and my father. I never felt closer to him than when we worked on the 'stang."

"I envied your relationship with your father. I felt as though my father didn't love us because I wasn't the boy he'd always wanted."

"That's ridiculous," Remy said.

"Was it?" Shelby opened her eyes long enough to shoot a glance his way. "He's since had two sons with the woman he married after divorcing my mother." She closed her eyes again. "He paid child support until I turned eighteen, but he rarely asked us to visit him and his new family. He didn't want us."

"You don't know that," Remy said.

She sighed. "We only hear from him on birthdays and Christmas—and I think it's his wife sending the cards. I learned a long time ago to rely on myself. No one else."

"I learned a long time ago in the Navy to help my brothers and sisters. I have their backs, and they have mine," Remy said. "No man is an island. We need each other to survive."

"Yeah," she said. "Well, I don't need anyone. I don't rely on anyone. It only leads to disappointment and hard times. I might not make much as a deputy, but I pay my bills. I can support myself and anyone who might come along."

"What if someone wants to be a part of your life, to share your world, both financially and emotionally?" Remy asked.

"So far, that hasn't happened," she said, sitting up straight and looking out at the road ahead. "I'm not sure I could relinquish control of my life to someone else. I never want to be in a situation where I'd be destitute if someone I loved and trusted left me."

Remy had been driving all the while they'd been talking. He pulled into the driveway of Broussard Country Store.

"I'll wait out here," Shelby said.

Remy exited the truck and rounded the front to the passenger side, opening the door.

"What are you doing?" Shelby asked.

"You're going in with me," he said.

She crossed her arms over her chest. "I don't need anything."

"I'm not leaving you out here. I can't keep an eye on you if you're not where I am." He cocked an eyebrow. "Now, are you coming in with me, or do I have to carry you in?"

Her eyes narrowed. "You wouldn't…would you?"

He leaned into the cab.

CHAPTER 10

Shelby threw up her hands. "Okay, okay. I'm getting out. Sheesh," she groused. "I'm tired. I don't feel like shopping,"

"I'm sorry to inconvenience you," he said.

"You don't look sorry," she grumbled as she slid out of the seat and into his arms.

He held her steady for a long moment, staring down into her eyes. "I'm not trying to make your life difficult. I only want you to be safe."

She sighed. "Okay, but five minutes max, and I'm out of here. I'm tired and way past being nice."

Remy cupped her elbow and led her through the front door of the store.

A bell rang over the door. "Welcome to Broussard's," a male voice called out.

"Hey, Alan, it's Shelby," she called out. "We just stopped for a minute to pick up a few groceries."

Gerard appeared in front of her. "Can I help you?"

Shelby stepped back, her eyes wide. "Wow, I wasn't expecting that."

Remy chuckled. "Way to scare the customers," he said.

Gerard frowned, "Sorry. I was stocking shelves one aisle over when I heard the bell. Thought I'd see who came through the door." He held out a hand to Remy. "How was the trip out to the boat wreck?"

"Depressing," Shelby answered. "We need a few things for the house. I haven't been shopping in over a week. My sister around?"

Alan joined them. "She's out. Had to run the oldest to his baseball practice. She took the ones who can walk. I have the baby in the back. He's sleeping. Do I need to call her?"

"No," Shelby said. "We aren't staying long. Just needed food for dinner and breakfast."

"Help yourself. I've got to fill an order for a customer who wants curbside service."

Remy secured a shopping cart and wheeled it in front of Shelby. "Hold onto this. I'll fill it."

Shelby pushed the cart, following Remy as he walked down the store's aisles. He didn't slow as he snagged cans of beans, tomato sauce, chicken broth and other staples and placed them into the cart.

He turned toward the refrigerator section, where he selected eggs, bacon, milk and orange juice. He paused in front of the meats. After a quick perusal, he selected packages of chicken, pork chops, sausage and steak.

Next stop was for fresh fruits and vegetables. Tomatoes, lettuce, celery, carrots, onions, apples, oranges, bananas and strawberries. "We'll hit the farmer's market on the weekend for watermelon and cantaloupe."

"That's enough food to feed an army. Are you planning on having guests over?" she asked.

"No, but we need to eat, and some of this can go in the freezer for later this week."

"You do realize someone has to cook this," she said.

"I know."

"Just so you know…" Shelby said. "While Chrissy was learning to cook, I was out fishing with my dad. I can burn boiled water. I can catch all the fish you can eat and filet it faster than most. But I wouldn't know whether you boil, bake or fry the catch."

Remy gave her a brief smile. "I can cook," he said.

Her eyes narrowed. "You spent your summers working on a car. When did you learn to cook?"

He grinned. "When we were at our home station, not deployed, my team got tired of eating out. So, we took turns cooking meals. Some guys preferred to grill everything. I liked making stuff my grandmother made when I was growing up. My mother sent me Gran's old Cajun cookbook. I've made almost everything in it."

Her eyebrows rose. "I'm impressed. Why hasn't some woman married you yet?"

His grin faded. "The life married to a Navy SEAL isn't for every woman. We were gone a lot. Most of the guys who were married ended up divorced. They missed babies being born, birthdays, watching their kid learn to walk, dance recitals and ball games." He added a bag of rice to the cart. "I never found someone I thought could put up with that kind of life. I wouldn't want to put her through it."

"What if she knew what she was getting into and was willing to put up with the absences?" Shelby asked.

"I wasn't willing to miss everything. Better to not have a family than to miss them." Which had led to a lot of lonely years. If not for his team, he might have been more miserable.

"You're retired now," Shelby said. "It's not too late. You're not too old to start a family. Men can sire children into their seventies. You'll need a younger wife, though. Childbearing years end sooner."

Remy chuckled. "Know any willing women who are looking to start a family?" He stopped in front of a freezer.

Shelby gave him a crooked smile. "Sure. But the ones in their thirties are usually divorced, with children. Are you willing to take on a package deal? If so, I know five women who would love a shot at a good-looking guy who hasn't let himself go."

Remy laughed. "So, I'm good-looking, am I?"

"Don't let it go to your head, please. Emphasis on *he hasn't let himself go.*"

"Are there any ladies who haven't married but aren't fresh out of high school or college? I'm not interested in a woman who could be my daughter."

Shelby drew in a deep breath. "Some of my friends might be interested."

"You'd be okay with me dating your friends?" Remy pulled out a carton of Rocky Road ice cream and one of vanilla. "Chocolate or vanilla?"

"Mint Chocolate Chip," she said.

He laughed. "Now, see? We would make a perfect couple."

"Why do you say that?"

"You like Mint Chocolate Chip ice cream."

"So? Is that your favorite?"

He shook his head. "I'm a big fan of Rocky Road."

Shelby grimaced. "I don't like marshmallows in my ice cream. It's just not natural."

"And I don't like mint in my ice cream." He put the vanilla back in the freezer and selected a Mint Chocolate Chip carton, placing it into the cart.

"I don't understand," she said. "How would that make us a perfect couple?"

"We'd never fight over the last bite of ice cream. Never steal the other's ice cream. Having things in common can be fatal to a relationship when it comes to ice cream."

Shelby's lips twitched.

Remy liked when she smiled. It brightened the room.

"Well," she said, "it's a good thing we're not a couple. One night, I might get desperate for chocolate ice cream, fish all the marshmallows out of the Rocky Road and finish the carton. Our relationship would end over an empty carton of Rock Road."

"That would be a shame. Because I bet we'd be compatible in all the ways that count."

"Like?"

"You like to fish. I don't know too many women who like to go fishing."

"There is that."

"Now that I'm retired from active duty, I'll have more time to work on cars. I know old engines and don't mind getting grease under my fingernails."

Shelby pushed the cart toward the checkout counter, where Alan was filling bags as he rang up the price of each item.

"A man who isn't afraid of getting grease under his fingernails is scarce these days..." she tilted her head to the side, "and strangely attractive."

"I'm getting better looking by the minute, right?"

He was teasing, but beneath the light banter, he was serious and hopeful that Shelby would see him as more than just her bodyguard or a one-night stand if she remembered that night.

"You two ready?" Alan asked as he placed the last item in a bag and printed out the receipt. "I have a few minutes before Madame Gautier gets here for her groceries."

Remy's brow wrinkled. "Madame Gautier, the Voodoo Queen?"

Alan nodded. "Yeah. I don't like to keep her waiting."

"I wouldn't either," Remy said. "She might put a spell on you."

"I know, right?" Alan shook his head. "I heard Willie Smithers got sideways with her, and she put a spell on him and made his willy wither."

Shelby laughed. "You don't believe that, do you?"

Alan and Remy both looked at her.

"I'm not willing to test her," Remy turned to Alan. "Are you?"

Alan shook his head. "No way."

"Then let's not hold up Madame Gautier," Shelby said. "I want to get home sometime before dark."

"On it," Alan said and rang up the items in the cart.

"Can you put it on my account," Shelby asked. "I don't have my credit card with me."

Remy removed a card from his wallet. "I'm getting this. I'll probably eat most of it."

"I can afford to buy groceries," Shelby said with a stubborn frown.

"I know," he said. "You can buy the next round. Deal?"

Alan took the card from Remy's hand. "Madame Gautier just pulled up. You two can duke it out later." He ran Remy's card and handed it back. "If you'll excuse me, I have to save my willy." Alan hefted the grocery bags he'd set aside on the counter and carried them out the front door.

Remy gathered theirs in both arms, leaving the lightest one for Shelby.

She took the bag and followed him out the door.

At her truck, Shelby set her bag in the middle of the seat. "I'll be just a minute."

Remy leaned into his side and deposited the bags next to Shelby's one, then watched her through the cab as she stepped up to the vintage Cadillac parked beside her. Alan was loading groceries into the trunk.

She spoke to the woman seated behind the wheel, wearing a brightly colored turban around her head and a matching caftan. Her mocha skin glistened in the heat. It had been twenty years since Remy had seen Madame Gautier, and she still made the hairs on his arms stand on end. Not that she'd done anything to make his willy wither, but he never wanted to take chances where she was concerned.

Shelby leaned back, giving Remy a clearer view of Bayou Mambaloa's resident Voodoo Queen.

She waved and smiled, her teeth gleaming white in her dark face.

Remy waved and smiled back, ready to go the moment Shelby got into the truck.

Alan finished loading the groceries and closed the trunk lid. "Thank you, Madame Gautier," he said as he passed behind Shelby. "Say hello to Gisele for me and Chrissy."

"I will," she called out. "Thank you, sonny."

Alan shot a glance toward Remy and ducked back into the store.

Remy slid into the driver's seat and closed the door, knowing it would be loud and, hopefully, a big hint to Shelby.

She looked over her shoulder, spoke to the older woman and finally climbed up into the truck, collapsing against the seat. "Okay. I cry uncle. Take me home."

Remy already had the truck in reverse and quickly backed out of the parking space beside Madame Gautier's. He glanced at Shelby.

Her eyes were closed.

He shifted into drive and pulled out onto Main Street. "Are you going to tell me what you two talked about?"

"No," Shelby said.

Remy frowned and drove a block before his

curiosity got the better of him. "Did you talk about your attack? Does she have any idea who might have done it? Or does she have a potion to magic up some suspects?"

Shelby turned her head and gave him an *are-you-serious* glare. "Yes. No. And no. If you must know, I was asking about her granddaughter, my friend, Gisele. I wanted to know if she's going to read tarot cards at the festival this weekend."

"She doesn't know who might've attacked you?"

"No, but she said I should talk to the Fontenots. They live on the bayou and take their fishing boats out into the gulf every day, as well as charter fishing trips and airboat rides for tourists. They're all over the bayou. If anyone has seen anything, they would have. And some of them are tight on funds, more than others in the family."

Remy glared at her. "Seriously? You weren't going to tell me that?"

She grinned. "I was. But I was curious how long you could stand it. I thought for sure you'd ask if she was putting a spell on your willy."

He gripped the steering wheel tightly. "You're an evil woman, Shelby Taylor."

"I'll take that as a compliment," she said smugly and turned to face the road, closing her eyes again.

His anger didn't last long. Not when she had that smug smile curling her lips. Even after having been attacked, she'd kept her sense of humor.

She didn't have to give him directions to her house. He remembered it from when he'd dated Chrissy in high school. He pulled into the driveway minutes later.

It was a small cottage with peeling paint and a bright royal blue front door. "That door was yellow the last time I was here," he said.

"That was twenty years ago," Shelby said. "I painted it when I took over the mortgage from my mother. I will have it paid off in a few years, and then it will be all mine."

"I like the blue," he said.

"I haven't had time to strip the old paint and repaint the rest of the house. But I will."

She didn't add the words *by myself,* but Remy could feel them implied.

Shelby stared at the cottage. "This was the only house my mother could afford after she and my father divorced. It wasn't the fanciest home in Bayou Mambaloa, but there are a lot of good memories in that house that I share with my mother and sister." She shrugged. "It's not much, but it's mine."

Remy shifted into park, turned the key, killing the engine, and pulled the key free. Before he could get out of his seat, Shelby was already opening her own door.

He jumped down and ran around to the other side of the old truck, arriving in time for Shelby to slide out of her seat. When her feet hit the ground, she would have fallen if not for holding onto the door.

Remy reached out to steady her.

She shook her head. "I can do this on my own."

"I'm sure you can," Remy said. "But it's easier to pick you up from a standing position than dragging you up off the ground."

He didn't wait for her to protest. Instead, he swept her into his arms and marched toward the front door.

"Seriously, I'm capable—"

"Shh," he interrupted her. "I'm concentrating on not dropping you."

"If I'm that heavy, put me down," she said.

"You're not heavy," he said. "You're talking too much. Now, hush while I negotiate these stairs."

She frowned heavily but shut up while he climbed the rickety stairs to the front door.

"Do you have a key to the door?" he asked. "Or do you hide it under a flowerpot?"

Her lips twisted. "Put me down."

He complied. Without a key, he couldn't go further. But he kept a hand around her waist in case her knees buckled again.

Shelby reached over the doorframe and came away with the key in her hand.

Remy's heart dropped into his belly. "Oh, sweetheart, you can't keep the key there anymore."

"Yeah," she said with a grimace. "I know. It sucks,

though. I used to think this town was a safe place to live."

"You've been a deputy here for how long?"

"Seven years."

"And you didn't deal with any crime during that time?" he asked.

She slipped the key into the lock and twisted. "Nothing directed at me, personally."

"Well, things change." He studied the door lock and nearly had a coronary. The lock on the doorknob was the only lock. No deadbolt. Holy shit. How did she stay safe? "While I'm here, we'll work on the lock situation."

"I already have," she said, holding up the key as she pushed the door inward.

Remy shook his head. "Not enough. You need deadbolts on your doors."

"Why?" she challenged. "If someone wanted in badly enough, all they'd have to do is break a window." Shelby entered the house.

"And you'll need a security system." He followed her inside and stopped her in the front entryway. "Stay."

She frowned. "I'm not a dog."

"You're right," he said. "A dog wouldn't argue with me. And a dog is a good idea. A big dog." He adjusted his tone to something more agreeable. "Please stay here while I check the premises."

"I can do that my—" she started.

Remy placed a finger over her lips. "I said please."

Her frown deepened. "Fine," she said around the finger over her lips.

He'd bet she'd thought about biting that finger. His lips twitched as he dropped his hand, closed the front door and quickly checked the house for intruders. When he returned to the front entryway, he caught a whole lot of attitude.

Shelby stood with her arms crossed over her chest, her eyebrows hiked. "Satisfied?"

He nodded. "All clear."

"I could have told you that," she said and moved into the living room with its floral, overstuffed sofa, mauve lounge chair and mismatched coffee table and end tables that probably came from completely different yard sales.

The furniture might be a little on the shabby side but it appeared to be comfortable and welcoming.

On his check through the house, he'd noted that the master bedroom had a queen-size bed with a maple headboard in the old farmhouse style from the late nineteen-nineties. The only newish item he'd been able to determine had been a white comforter and pillows covered in crisp white pillowcases.

The guest bedroom was a study in powder-blue curtains with a matching blue comforter covered in a white and yellow daisy pattern. The double bed was nothing more than a metal bedframe with a mattress and box spring. No headboard. Over the bed hung a print of a field of daisies with a light blue summer sky background.

The third bedroom was full of boxes and old furniture.

"You can sleep in the daisy room," Shelby said.

"Who needs Madame Gautier's potions to shrink your willy when you can sleep in a frou-frou bedroom meant for a little girl?" he muttered.

"What was that?" Shelby asked.

"Nothing. The daisy room beats a foxhole any day. I'll get the groceries." He left her in the house and returned to her truck to gather the groceries, shaking his head as he did. He'd be glad when his truck made it down from Montana. Power steering and air-conditioning made all the difference in southern Louisiana's heat and humidity.

He carried the grocery bags into the house and set them down in the kitchen.

Shelby wasn't in the living room or kitchen. He walked toward the master bedroom. The door to her bedroom was open, and the inner door to the bathroom was closed. When he heard the sound of the shower, he nodded.

Good. He had time to make dinner. A sure way to impress a woman was a man who could cook. Or so his buddies had said. He hadn't tried the skill on a female. His cooking skills had been honed trying to one-up his brothers-in-arms. And out of self-preservation. Eating out got old and packed on pounds he didn't need to lug into battle. Not that he was heading into battle…well, not the kinds of battle he'd faced before.

While Shelby showered, Remy whipped up a rue in a stock pot. Then he sauteed onions, carrots and celery with Cajun seasoning. After cutting chicken tenderloins and cooking them in olive oil in a skillet, he poured everything into the large stock pot with chicken broth, tail-less shrimp and smoked sausage and let it simmer. He put on a pot of water to boil for rice and added a touch of salt. Once the water boiled, he poured in the rice and stirred it to keep it from sticking to the bottom.

He remembered his grandmother doing all of this, moving from her cutting board to the stove, the sink and the refrigerator in a graceful dance of cooking with love for her family.

When the rice was ready, he covered it and turned the heat down on the gumbo.

Shelby hadn't emerged from her room. He left the kitchen to check on her and make sure she hadn't fallen.

The door to her bedroom was still open, and the door to the bathroom stood open as well. A movement caught his attention. A full-length mirror leaned against a wall across from a closet.

Shelby's reflection was what had caught his attention. She stood in the closet with a towel wrapped around her middle, staring at the clothes on the hangers.

She must have found what she was looking for because she reached for a hanger, dropping the towel in the process.

Remy's breath caught in his throat.

She stretched up for the hanger, her naked body pure art in all the lines and curves. Every one of which Remy had touched when they'd spent that stormy night together in the fishing hut.

Frozen in time, he couldn't move, couldn't look away.

Shelby tugged a pale blue dress from a hanger, lifted it and pulled it over her head. She turned just enough to expose a perfect breast.

Remy forgot to breathe, to think, to move.

The soft fabric drifted down over her body, molding to her form, the hem falling to the middle of her thighs. She bent to step into a pair of lacy underwear and pulled the garment over her naked ass.

At that moment, she turned toward the mirror.

Too late. By the time Remy realized his reflection was in that same mirror, she'd seen him.

"Uh…" he said so eloquently. "Are you ready?"

Her eyes widened.

"For dinner," he added.

"Yes," she said, smoothing her hand over the dress.

Remy's cock jerked. "Need any help?" he asked a

little late since she was already showered and dressed.

Her lips curled on the corners. "Not now."

His cock growing harder by the second, Remy nodded. "Then I'll be in the kitchen." He spun before he did something she wasn't ready for.

"Remy?" Shelby's voice called out.

He half-turned, unwilling to expose the extent of his erection. "Yes?"

Her brow dipped slightly. "How long have you been standing there?"

He sighed, unwilling to lie. "Long enough."

She met his gaze for a long moment. "And?"

"Sweet Jesus, Shelby, what do you want me to say? Sorry, isn't it. I'm not sorry I saw you. You're beautiful." He shook his head. "I'm not sorry I saw you at all. So, sue me." He turned and headed back to the kitchen, opened the refrigerator door and stood in the cool air, fighting a losing battle over his instinctive reaction to her beautiful body.

He wanted so badly to take her into his arms, rip the dress over her head and drive deep into her.

But she didn't remember they'd made love before. If he came on to her now, she'd freak. When they made love again, he wanted her to be just as aroused as he was, just as free with her body as she'd been the time before.

Remy was nowhere near collected by the time Shelby emerged from her bedroom and joined him in the small kitchen. The kitchen was small for one person, impossible for two unless they were willing to slide against each other in a sensuous dance.

Yet, Shelby entered, nevertheless, the body that had been naked moments before, now clad in the pale blue dress, squeezed behind him, her hips brushing against his, her breasts sliding across his back.

A groan rose in Remy's throat. He swallowed hard to keep it from escaping.

When she reached around him to open a drawer and retrieve spoons, her breast brushed against his arm, her pelvis bumping against his buttocks.

That groan escaped.

Shelby stopped moving. "Are you all right?"

He spun and gripped her arms in his hands. "This kitchen is too small for two people."

She stared up into his eyes. "Obviously."

"Can I get something for you?"

She held up two spoons and gave him a hint of a smile, her eyelids at half-mast. "I got what I came for."

If she'd come to get him all hot and bothered, she'd accomplished her mission. "Sit at the table. I'll bring the gumbo to you," he said in a gruff voice.

"Yes, sir," she said with a saucy grin. She turned. As she left the kitchen with her spoons, she deliberately brushed his arm with her breasts.

Remy leaned his head back, holding his breath until Shelby exited the kitchen.

While she set the table with placemats, silverware and glasses, Remy scooped rice into two bowls and layered gumbo over the top. He carried the bowls to the small dining table and set them on the placemats.

"Mmm," Shelby sniffed. "Just like Madame Gautier makes."

He frowned. "The Voodoo Queen made you gumbo?"

"She did."

Remy held a chair for Shelby. "You said you're friends with her granddaughter?"

Shelby sank into the seat. "I am."

"Does your friend practice Voodoo as well?"

"Some." Shelby lifted her spoon. "But she doesn't advertise the fact. People get all weird when you tell them you practice Voodoo. A lot of it is just working with natural remedies."

"And shrinking willy spells." Remy shook his head as he took his seat across from Shelby. "Remind me not to get sideways with either one of them."

"You really believe in all that magic?"

"No, but I prefer to hedge my bets and play it safe."

Shelby grinned, dipped her spoon into the gumbo, took a small bite and moaned.

The sound had Remy's cock straining against his jeans. Thankfully, he was seated.

Shelby ate half the bowl of gumbo before laying

down her spoon. "It's so good, but I can't keep my eyes open."

"Go to bed," Remy said.

"You cooked," she said. "I should clean."

He shook his head. "You're still recovering. I'll take care of the kitchen. You should sleep."

She yawned. "I'm not going to argue."

"That's refreshing," he said with a grin as he gathered his bowl and hers and headed into the kitchen.

"Smart ass," she muttered as she pushed to her feet. "The sheets are clean in the daisy room, and there are fresh towels in the guest bathroom. Make yourself at home. I'm done for the night." She stood at the entrance to the kitchen, her eyelids drooping. "Thank you for dinner. I haven't had a home-cooked meal since the last time Chrissy invited me over."

After he set the bowls on the counter, he crossed to her. "You're welcome. My grandmother thought good food and sleep could cure anything."

"She was a smart woman." Shelby touched his chest. "Thanks for being here. I might not have shown my appreciation, but I am glad you're here."

He brushed a strand of her hair back behind her ear. "I'm glad I'm here, too." He bent and brushed his lips across hers.

Her hand rose from his chest to circle the back of his neck, bringing him closer.

She opened to him, and he thrust in, tangling his tongue with hers.

Remy could get lost in Shelby so easily.

He broke it off first, gripped her arms and set her away. "Go to bed."

She blinked up at him, her mouth opening and then closing. Finally, she nodded. "Good night." Shelby turned and hurried to her bedroom, closing the door between them.

As soon as she did, Remy spun toward the kitchen and spent the next thirty minutes dumping gumbo into containers, scrubbing pots and pans and drying every last drop off their surfaces. He cleaned the stovetop, ran a rag across the counter and looked for anything else he could do to keep busy.

The kitchen was clean. It was dark outside, or he'd mow the lawn and edge the sidewalk. No matter how hard he worked, he couldn't quit thinking about Shelby and that kiss.

Why had he stopped and sent her to her bed?

Alone?

A knock sounded on the front door.

Remy grabbed his gun from the counter where he'd placed it before he'd started cooking and approached the front door. Moving into the living room, he peered around the edge of the window to find a man standing on the stoop with a large bag slung over his shoulder. The man turned his head toward the streetlight.

Alan. Shelby's brother-in-law.

Remy opened the door. "Hey, Alan."

Alan nodded a greeting. "Remy. Gerard had me bring this to you. Thought you might need your things. He would've come but thought it better to stay with Chrissy and the kids."

"Great. Thanks." Remy took the duffel bag from the other man.

Alan frowned. "You really think Chrissy and the kids are in danger?"

"We don't know. But better safe than sorry, right?"

Alan nodded. "Yeah. I don't like it. The sooner they find the guys who attacked Shelby, the better." His eyes narrowed as he met Remy's gaze. "Shelby's family. I love my family and don't want anything bad to happen to them."

Remy got the message. *Don't fuck with Shelby.* "I care about Shelby. I don't want anyone to hurt her either."

He tipped his head back as if weighing the truth of Remy's declaration. Finally, he said, "Good. I feel better knowing you're looking out for her. And thanks for sending Gerard to help me look after Chrissy and the kids. Call me if you need me for anything." Alan didn't wait for a response. He walked back to his minivan, climbed in and drove away.

For a long moment, Remy's gaze followed the man in the minivan. He'd come to deliver Remy's things and a message to treat Shelby right.

Some men would take offense to such a warning. Not Remy. He liked that Chrissy's husband cared about his wife's sister. That meant more people were looking out for her.

He closed the door, locked it and found a wooden chair to brace under the door handle. He took another chair to the back door and wedged it under the door handle. Then he went around the house, checking all the window latches to ensure each was secure.

When he came to Shelby's bedroom door, he tapped softly.

No answer.

Careful not to make a noise, he turned the doorknob and opened the door.

Light from the hallway cast a beam across the floor to the bed where she lay, her eyes closed.

Remy entered her room and checked the latches on her bedroom window and the one in the bathroom.

When he emerged, movement from the bed caught his attention.

Shelby's arms and legs twitched, and her head moved from side to side. Her brow furrowed, tears slipping from the corners of her eyes, and her mouth opened on a low moan.

Remy's heart pinched hard in his chest. He bent over her and touched her shoulder. "Shelby, honey, wake up."

Her eyes remained closed, her movements becoming more desperate. "No," she whispered.

Remy gathered her stiff body into his arms and sat on the side of the bed. "Hey, sweetheart, it's okay. I've got you."

Her eyes blinked open, glazed and fearful.

"It's me, Remy," he said. "I've got you now. No one is going to hurt you."

She pressed her face to his chest and curled her fingers into his shirt.

Remy kicked off his boots and scooted further onto the bed, settling back against the pillows. He held her close as the nightmare passed, and her body relaxed against his.

As much as he wanted to be with Shelby, he didn't want it to be because she was scared and grateful he was looking out for her. He never wanted her to mistake gratitude for love.

He hadn't taken the kiss further because he thought she wasn't ready. Hell, maybe he wasn't ready, or the time wasn't right. She'd told him she never wanted to be dependent on a man, that she wanted to be able to stand on her own.

Could he convince her he wanted to be with her as a partner and that he would never compromise her independence?

Whatever he had to do, he would. She was worth the effort. He'd never met anyone as strong and independent as Shelby Taylor.

He had her where he wanted her, in his arms, but he wanted more than just to hold her. He wanted to love her and for her to love him unconditionally.

If that meant holding her and not making love to her to prove he wasn't just after the one-night stand she couldn't remember, so be it. One thing was certain, he had a long night ahead of him, holding the woman he wanted more than he wanted to breathe and not making love to her.

Yeah, it was going to be a long…hard…night.

CHAPTER 11

SHELBY WOKE the next morning feeling well-rested and just *good* all over. She'd had a bad dream about being trapped in the marsh grass, the reeds pulling at her legs and taking her deep into the water. Just when her head went under, strong arms pulled her out of the water and wrapped her in a warm, dry blanket.

She knew without seeing his face that it was Remy. He'd saved her from drowning and held her until she fell into a dreamless sleep.

When she'd opened her eyes to morning, she'd half-expected to see him lying in the bed beside her. She couldn't deny the disappointment tugging at her heart when the space beside her was empty.

A glance at the clock on her nightstand made her eyes widen. Hell, she'd slept longer than she had in years. Half the morning was gone.

The sounds of pots and pans clanking in the kitchen reassured her that he was still in her house. The scent of bacon frying made her stomach rumble. She threw back the covers and rolled out of bed, careful to make sure her legs would hold her before she got too cocky.

Her legs held steady as she stood, and she didn't have even a hint of dizziness. Hell, she could go back to work today if the doctor hadn't grounded her for two weeks.

Maybe the two weeks' leave was just what she needed. Not to recover so much as to discover. She'd have time to figure out who the hell had attacked her. So she'd better make good use of that time and shut down the bastards before they hurt someone else.

Shelby hurried into the bathroom, closed the door and washed her face, brushed her hair and pulled it back into her usual ponytail. After a quick glance in the mirror, she yanked the elastic band out of her hair, brushed it smooth and applied a little blush to her pale cheeks and mascara to her eyelashes.

She didn't normally wear makeup on the job. Why bother? She'd sweat it off in the heat and humidity.

Then why are you bothering now?

The devil on her shoulder demanded an answer.

"Because I'm not going to work," she muttered to the woman in the mirror.

Because you have a sexy bodyguard in your house who has only seen you at your worst.

"Yeah, okay, fine. He's sexy, and he kisses like nobody's business."

"Shelby, are you all right?" Remy's voice sounded on the other side of the door.

Shelby opened the door to find him standing there with an oven mitt on one hand and a frown denting his forehead.

"I'm fine. Why do you ask?"

"I came to tell you breakfast is ready, and I heard you talking to someone." He looked over her shoulder into the bathroom.

She gave him a crooked smile. "Sometimes, I talk to myself."

His frown cleared. "I do that too when I'm trying to get my shit together. Did the conversation come out all right?"

Her cheeks burned. "Yeah." She sniffed the air. "Is that bacon I smell?

"It is," he grinned. "And I made omelets and biscuits."

She chuckled. "Just a regular Martha Stewart, aren't you?"

"I like to think of myself as more of a Gordon Ramsay. I don't look good in a dress."

Shelby laughed at the image she conjured of Remy, with his broad shoulders, in a dress. "I don't know. With the right heels, I think you could pull it off." She stepped past him on her way to the good smells coming from the other part of the house.

"I'll pass on the heels and the dress, but I'm not giving up on kitchen duty. I like to cook what I like to eat. You're just the lucky recipient of the extra ingredients."

Remy had set the table with two plates filled with fluffy omelets, a plate full of bacon and a basket filled with fluffy biscuits.

He held her chair.

"I could get used to this," she murmured as she sat.

"Orange juice or coffee?"

"Both," she answered.

He entered the kitchen and was back in seconds with a mug of coffee and a glass of orange juice. "Thought you might like both."

He took his seat across from her.

Shelby tucked into the food hungrier than she'd thought. When she'd polished off the last of her omelet and a biscuit slathered with strawberry jam, she leaned back in her chair. "Wow, that was amazing. I don't think I need to eat again for a week."

"You needed it," he said and gathered their plates.

She rose to help, carrying the basket of biscuits.

They worked side-by-side at the sink, him washing, her drying. Each time her shoulder or hip bumped his, a blast of heat rushed through her. Imagining those arms wrapped around her body, holding her close, sent that heat lower, coiling at her core. By the time they'd finished cleaning the kitchen, she wanted to take his hand and lead him back to the bedroom.

He hung the dishtowel and turned toward her.

Shelby raised her hand.

Before he could take it, a knock sounded at her front door.

Shelby frowned and dropped her hand. "Who the hell could that be?" She turned and hurried toward the front door.

Remy quickly caught her arm. "Let me."

She frowned but backed away as he went first to the living room window and peered around the edge. "There's a young woman with dark hair, dark eyes and dark skin at the door."

Shelby smiled. "Sounds like Gisele." She reached for the doorknob and pulled open the door.

Her petite friend flew through the door and wrapped her arms around Shelby in a breath-stealing hug. "Shelby, my dear friend. What were you thinkin' goin' 'round the bayou alone?"

Shelby laughed. "That I was doing my job?" She extricated herself from her friend's tight hold. "I'm all right."

"But they took you to the hospital in the city. Grand-mère says that hospital has bad juju."

"She may have been right."

Gisele nodded. "Seriously?"

Shelby nodded. "Someone tried to smother me while I was lying in a coma."

"They should've brought you to Grand-mère." Gisele took her hands. "She loves you like her own."

"That's very sweet of her," Shelby said. "Please thank her for thinking of me." She stared at her friend. "What brings you here?'

"Do I need a reason to visit my friend who has been brutalized?"

"Not at all," Shelby hugged Gisele again. "But you look like a woman on a mission."

"I am," she admitted. "Grand-mère wanted you to know the Fontenots are having a party at their compound in the bayou for Pierre Fontenot, who is celebrating his one hundredth birthday. All the Fontenots and their friends will be there tonight. You'll have all of them in one place to ask questions about the night you were attacked."

"Tonight?" Shelby asked. "Do you have to be invited?"

Gisele shook her head. "No, but it's polite to take a covered dish. They're having a crawfish and crab boil, and some of the cousins are in a zydeco band."

Shelby looked to Remy.

He nodded. "We can go. I can whip up something edible to take with us."

Shelby smiled. "Thanks."

Gisele hugged Shelby again. "I'm glad you're doing better. You scared us all."

"I'm not going anywhere anytime soon. They haven't got me down yet."

"Good." Gisele hugged her again. "I have to get the gift shop open, or I'd stay longer. I'll see you two tonight."

"You'll be there?" Shelby asked.

"Wouldn't miss it," Gisele smiled. "Love me some zydeco music, and I want to keep an eye on my cousin Lissette. She's been stirring up trouble lately, using some of Grand-mère's potions for bad juju."

Shelby frowned. "Should I be concerned?"

"Only if you're a man. She's trying out love potions on unsuspecting dudes. When it doesn't work out, she gives them swamp warts."

Shelby shot a glance toward Remy. "Should Remy be worried?"

The man's hand slipped low to cover his crotch. "Yeah, should I be worried?"

Gisele laughed, the sound as light and beautiful as the woman. "Not as long as you carry a gris-gris to protect you." She dug into the pocket of her colorful dress, pulled out a tiny cloth bag and handed it to Remy. "Carry this with you at all times."

His brow wrinkled as he took the bag about the size of a quarter and held it up to his nose. "What's in it?"

Gisele's pretty smile disappeared as she donned her Voodoo priestess role she used when selling items in her Mamba Wamba gift shop to tourists.

"Ingredients designed to protect the one who carries it."

Shelby almost laughed at the way Remy's eyes rounded.

While Remy looked down at the bag in his hand, Gisele winked at Shelby.

"See you tonight," Gisele said and left.

Remy's gaze followed Gisele out to the scooter she climbed aboard and turned out onto the street. As she took off, her long, flowing skirt flared out behind her. She looked like a beautiful witch taking off on her broom. Only it wasn't a broom but her beloved Vespa.

Shelby touched Remy's arm. "She's a good Voodoo priestess-in-training with her grandmother."

"And the cousin?" he asked, rubbing the cloth bag between his thumb and fingers.

"Lissette has always been a wild thing," Shelby said. "Her father, Madame Gautier's son, disappeared when Lissette was little, and her mother has bounced from relationship to relationship, leaving Lissette alone so often she pretty much raised herself."

"That doesn't bode well for her own ability to maintain a good relationship with anyone, male or female."

Shelby nodded. "Exactly. Madame Gautier tried to bring her under her wing several times, but her mother refused to let her stay long enough for her grandmother to be a good influence. Instead, she picked up some of Madame Gautier's spells and potions for not-so-good uses."

"Again, should we be worried?"

"Only if you believe in all that mumbo jumbo," Shelby said.

"I'd rather believe and take precautions than suffer the consequences."

Shelby grinned. "Welcome home to the bayou, Remy."

He sighed. "I'd forgotten how superstitious people could be here."

Shelby closed the front door and turned to him. "It's all part of the charm of Bayou Mambaloa." She planted her fists on her hips. "So, what's the plan for today? Are we going back out into the bayou to poke around?"

"Since we're going to poke around at the Fontenots' in the bayou this evening, I thought we might look around town for a place to set up shop for my Bayou Brotherhood Protectors. They'll be heading south soon, and I want to be ready with lodging and have a site nailed down for our offices, both temporary and permanent."

"You need a real estate agent? LaShawnda Jones is good. I'll give her a call and set up a time for us to meet."

"Sounds good. And while we're out, we can look around town for places that could work as drug distribution sites. You never know, the traffickers could be working right under our noses."

Shelby nodded. "I was thinking the same. This town used to be larger than it is now, with a booming fishing industry and businesses that supported fishing and the people who worked here." Her lips turned downward. "It's a shame when a town or parts of it die. Most of the young people migrate to larger cities to find work and never come back."

Remy nodded. "I noticed that there are more stores and restaurants open since I left twenty years ago."

Shelby smiled. "Tourism has helped to revive much of Bayou Mambaloa. Over the years, the town council has come up with more ways to draw visitors. We have annual music festivals and parades, and we advertise the beauty and mysteriousness of the bayou."

"How soon can we get with your real estate agent?" Remy asked.

"I'll give her a call now. I can be ready in fifteen minutes."

"I only need five," he said with a grin. "If we can't see your friend right away, we can drive around looking for now."

They split up and went to their separate bathrooms.

Shelby called LaShawnda, who had immediate availability. She'd contact sellers, arrange to see available buildings and meet them in the town square in fifteen minutes.

"Perfect," Shelby said. "See ya there."

Fifteen minutes later, Shelby and Remy parked the truck in the town square beside a sleek black SUV.

LaShawnda stepped out dressed in a tangerine pantsuit, matching long-tipped acrylic fingernails and chunky gold jewelry around her neck and wrists. Her thick hair was straight with streaks of auburn hanging down to her shoulders, and she wore Hollywood sunglasses.

"Shelby, darling." She stepped forward in bright gold strappy three-inch heels. "I heard you ran into some trouble in the bayou." She wrapped her arms around Shelby and hugged her briefly. "I'm glad to see you're recovering nicely. I don't know what this community would do without you and the rest of the sheriff's department to protect us."

"Thank you, LaLa," she said. "It's good to see you. You've been gone for a couple of weeks, right?"

"I have. I went to a Real Estate convention in Atlanta. But I'm back and ready to put my knowledge to work." She turned to Remy with a big, beautiful smile. "And who is this scrumptious man? Please tell me he's single."

"Remy, this is LaShawnda Jones. LaLa, do you remember Remy Montagne? He was in high school with Chrissy when we were still in junior high."

One well-sculpted brow lifted. "You're the Remy Chrissy dated in high school?" She held out her hand. "Whatever you've been up to since, keep doing it. You look amazing. Are you in town for long?"

He nodded. "I'm here to stay. That's why we need your help."

"Shelby gave me a heads-up on what you're looking for. But now, Shelby…" LaShawnda's gaze went from Remy to Shelby and back, "Will you be looking for a bigger home? Maybe one with four or five bedrooms for your babies?"

Shelby's cheeks burned. "No, this isn't about me. Besides, you know I don't have any babies. Remy is looking for a place to house his business and the staff he will employ."

"Such a shame. I'd like to get my girl, Shelby, into a bigger house for all the right reasons." LaShawnda winked, then cocked one eyebrow as she looked toward Remy. "Well then, what kind of building are you looking for, and what kind of business will be conducted there?"

"I'm looking for a small manufacturing facility to build custom pirogues," Remy said.

LaShawnda nodded. "I have some ideas for that."

"I also need a place for my guys to live when they come to work for me until they can find their own homes. There could be up to ten at one time."

LaShawnda's eyes narrowed. "That might be more challenging. But I know of a couple of places that might fit your needs. You might have to move on them quickly as another buyer in the area is looking for a manufacturing facility."

"Really?" Shelby said. "Since when is Bayou Mambaloa a mecca for manufacturing?"

LaShawnda shrugged. "Could be the skyrocketing prices of property in New Orleans. Since we're not that far from the city, we might be a better option."

"True," Remy said. "We've been looking in New Orleans and Baton Rouge. When we find something that might work, it becomes a bidding war, or someone offers and is accepted before we have the opportunity."

LaShawnda nodded. "I've heard from some of my counterparts in New Orleans that the market is hot. Properties can be sold within a day of posting it on the MLS." She waved toward her vehicle. "Would you like to ride with me?"

"No," Shelby said.

"Yes," Remy countered and raised an eyebrow toward Shelby. "Miss Jones' vehicle is air-conditioned."

"Fine," Shelby said. "Yes, please, LaLa. We'd love to ride with you."

LaShawnda opened the back door.

"I'll sit in the back," Shelby said. "Remy's the client. He needs to see." She climbed into the SUV behind the driver's seat.

Remy rounded the vehicle and slid into the front passenger seat.

LaShawnda drove through town and turned south onto a road with a few small houses and a larger home with plain white paint, a wrap-around porch and upper balcony, and a small parking lot in front. She parked in front and nodded toward the big home. "This is the Henderson House. It was built by Robert Henderson back in the late eighteen hundreds for his family. The man had fourteen children. It has ten rooms and five bathrooms." She glanced toward Remy. "Would something like this work?"

Remy nodded. "Yes."

"Then let's go look." LaShawnda opened her door and stepped down from the vehicle.

Remy got out and came around to Shelby's side to open the door for her.

She got out and fell in step with the realtor.

Shawnda walked up the front steps to the door where a lockbox hung. "It's currently unoccupied. The owner had been running it as a bed-and-breakfast but has fallen ill and can't manage it anymore." She opened the lockbox, extracted the key and unlocked the front door.

She stood back and waved them inside. "It might need some updates, but everything works, and the last owner had the electricity and plumbing brought up to current code. He wants to sell the building as is, complete with furniture and appliances. Basically, it would be turnkey, ready to use."

Shelby followed Remy through the house, looking into each room that had been tastefully decorated in a mix of antique furniture and more modern pieces that blended well.

"The owner tried to stay true to the era in which this house was built, as much as possible—with the exception of the kitchen." LaShawnda led the way through the dining room into the kitchen.

Where the rest of the house had that old-world charm, the kitchen was filled with gleaming, stainless-steel appliances, countertops and modern conveniences, to include a commercial-grade dishwasher and refrigerator.

"I'd buy this house for the kitchen alone," LaShawnda said. "The owner was also a chef. He'd had dreams of making the entire first floor into a restaurant. By the time he finished outfitting the kitchen, he was running out of money, so he opened the bed and breakfast and put the restaurant on hold. He ran the bed and breakfast until his health failed, and he moved out to Phoenix to be close to his daughter. He's a motivated seller."

"Good to know," Remy said.

"Look around," LaShawnda said. "I'll be in the front parlor if you have questions."

"Thank you," Remy said, holding the door open for Shelby to pass back into the dining room.

He went from room to room on the first floor, taking pictures with his cell phone. Then he climbed the stairs to the second floor, checking each room, looking at the ceilings, floors and bathrooms, recording each room with a photo on his cell phone.

Shelby followed, admiring how the owner had furnished the old house with white iron beds, shiny brass beds, antique dressers and nightstands. The bathrooms had been updated with walk-in showers, new toilets, countertops and sinks.

"She's right," Shelby said. "This place is turnkey."

Remy nodded. "I don't see any signs of a leaky roof or water damage to the wooden floors from leaky plumbing. This place would work as a place to house our team. There's a decent-sized parlor we could use as our war room and a study we can convert into an armory until we can find and remodel a building for our main offices."

Shelby nodded. "Ready to move on to the next property LaShawnda has lined up?"

Remy nodded. "I want to look around the exterior, and then I'll be ready to move on."

Shelby followed him to the first floor. They found LaShawnda in the parlor, checking her emails on her cell phone.

She walked with them outside and around the building. The lot had become a little overgrown, but nothing that couldn't be fixed easily.

Remy turned to the agent. "I'll need you to send

me the information on this property in an email I can forward to my boss."

LaShawnda nodded, glanced down at her phone, punched several keys, hit send and then glanced up. "Done."

Remy smiled. "This will work for lodging and temporary office space. What do you have in the way of manufacturing space?"

Shelby grinned when LaShawnda spun on her gold heels. "Follow me." The ultimate professional, she had Shelby in awe of her poise and beauty. Especially since she remembered the little girl she'd played with in the mud growing up. She was so proud of her friend and her success as a real estate agent.

They climbed into the SUV and continued down the road another half mile to a long building perched on the edge of the bayou with its own dock. Made of metal, the building appeared to be holding up well for having been abandoned.

LaShawnda parked in the lot in front of the building. "This building was erected in 1959 for the Bayou Boat Factory. They built small skiffs, jon boats and pirogues that they sold throughout Louisiana and neighboring states."

They got out of the vehicle and followed LaShawnda to the door. It took her several tries to get the lockbox open. When she opened the door, the hinges squealed. "This building has stood empty for a decade. At the very least, it would require the new owner to upgrade the electrical system to code. The bank owns the land and building. Like I said, there's someone else interested, but they've yet to make a formal offer. Feel free to look around. I'll be out here if you have any questions."

Remy entered the building.

In the dimly lit interior, Shelby followed, picking her way carefully through old pallets, piles of twisted sheet metal and junk she didn't recognize. To her, the place needed to be bulldozed and hauled off.

After Remy made it all the way through the building, checking out the old office space and bathrooms, he exited through a side door that led to the dock.

Shelby joined him there, careful to tread lightly on the wooden planks.

Not Remy. He bounced on the wood. "I'm surprised how well this old dock has held up for having been abandoned for so long."

"I remember when they used to make boats here," Shelby said. "I was sad to come home from college to find out they'd shut down. The people who worked here either left town to find work or stayed but never found jobs that paid as well."

"The exterior bones appear to be good," Remy said. "No matter what we find, we'll have to renovate to make it work for our needs. I like the idea of having a real manufacturing business as a cover for our guys being here. It will also give them something to do when they're in between assignments."

"What do any of you know about making boats?"

"Not much," Remy said. "But my father worked as a foreman here until he retired and moved to Florida. That was right before they closed the factory. I bet I could get him on as a consultant to help us set up a small manufacturing line. He's bored out of his mind in retirement."

"It would be nice to see him again," Shelby said. "And your mother."

Remy grinned. "You know my mother would come if my father's here for any amount of time exceeding a week."

Shelby gazed out at the bayou, thinking of old times when Remy's parents and her mother had lived there.

Perhaps it was better that they didn't now, especially with potential drug runners making themselves at home in the bayou.

Shelby stared at the dock and the water beyond. "This would be a good place for a drug drop. It's out of sight of the town, has a dock and a storage facility to hold the stash until it's sold."

Remy nodded. "I was thinking the same thing. If it remains unsold and unoccupied, we need to keep an eye on it."

Shelby nodded. "I'll let the sheriff know. He can have a deputy check it once or twice a week."

"That would be a good idea. We don't want the drug trafficking to get any closer to town if we can help it."

Shelby shot him a smile. "So, have you made up your mind? Is this the place?"

Remy shrugged. "We need to look some more." He took her hand and walked back into the building, closing and securing the side door before leading Shelby back across the floor littered with junk.

LaShawnda took them to see several other places that might work for the lodging and manufacturing facility. None of them worked as well for Remy's needs as the Henderson House and the old boat factory.

When they returned to the town square, Remy stepped away from the two women and called his boss in Montana.

LaShawnda nodded toward Remy. "Are you two a thing?" she asked Shelby.

Shelby's gaze fixed on Remy. "I don't think so," she said.

LaShawnda's dark face split into a bright, white smile. "Girl, he's a hunk. You should be with him."

"I don't know. He might not be all that interested in me," Shelby shrugged. "He could have anyone he chooses. Why would he want to be with me?"

LaShawnda hugged Shelby. "Because you deserve your own happiness. You're the nicest, most loyal person I know. What's not to love?"

REMY

"A dog could get a better recommendation," Shelby grumbled. "I don't think he's interested."

"Seriously," LaShawnda said, "your man is interested. You don't see the way he looks at you when you're not looking." Her friend's smile softened. "He's into you. The question is, what are you going to do about it?"

"Nothing," Shelby said. "He's only here to protect me."

Remy finished his phone conversation with Hank and rejoined the two women. He locked gazes with LaShawnda. "How soon can you draw up the offers for the boarding house and the old boat factory?" Remy asked.

Lashawnda smiled. "I can have them written by the end of day."

"Good." He told her what he wanted to offer for the Henderson House and the boat factory. "And if you know a reputable contractor in the area, I'd like to get some work started on the renovations of the boat factory." Remy held out his hand. "Thank you for your help and patience."

"It was my pleasure." LaShawnda took his hand and shook it. "Will you be available later this afternoon?"

Remy shook his head. "Can it wait until morning? We have to be somewhere at five-thirty."

"I can have it to you before then," LaShawnda said. "Like I told you, someone else has been looking at the boat factory with another agent. I don't know if they've made an offer to the bank. If you want to follow me back to my office or wait an hour before you come by, I'll draw up the contract now. You can sign it, and I'll present it to the bank holding the note this afternoon."

"An hour?" Remy asked.

The agent nodded.

"Okay," Remy said. "We'll come by your office in an hour."

LaShawnda climbed into her SUV and drove away.

Remy glanced down at Shelby. "Hungry?"

Shelby glanced at her watch, surprised it was already one o'clock. Her stomach rumbled, and she laughed. "I guess I am."

"We can go back to your house, and I can cook something," he suggested. "I need to prepare something for the Fontenot's shindig."

"Will an hour be enough?" she asked.

"We can make lunch and decide what we'll take with us tonight." Remy held open the passenger door of her truck.

Shelby and Remy returned to her house and made sandwiches with deli meat, cheese, lettuce and tomatoes. They decided on taking cornbread and baked beans and laid out the ingredients for when they got back from signing the papers.

By the time they got to the real estate agent's

office, LaShawnda had the offers prepared with the amounts Remy had agreed on. He signed the documents and thanked LaShawnda for her prompt work.

"I'll let you know what I hear as soon as they make a decision." The agent smiled. "Cross your fingers."

Shelby crossed her fingers. If the deals went through, Remy was one step closer to staying in Bayou Mambaloa for good.

She couldn't stop the joy from welling in her chest at the thought of Remy being around on a permanent basis.

Now that they'd gotten him squared away with a lodging alternative and a place he could convert into headquarters for the Bayou Brotherhood Protectors, they could return their focus to catching a killer. Hopefully, they'd learn something at the Fontenot's party that evening.

If they were that familiar with everything going on in the bayou, they ought to have seen something that would lead Shelby to the people or person who'd attacked her.

She looked forward to talking with the family. They needed to find the local connection who could be working with the cartel if the cartel was actually involved with those who'd attacked her.

Shelby hoped they'd find that connection before whoever had tried to kill her tried again with better success.

CHAPTER 12

REMY and Shelby arrived at Pierre Fontenot's home in the bayou via the boat Mitch had set aside for them to rent.

The boat had a bigger engine, getting them there a lot faster than the boat they'd used the day before.

Dusk had settled in, casting the dock in deep shadows. Several boats were already tied to the moorings when Remy helped Shelby out of the boat onto the dock. She held the cornbread wrapped in foil. Remy carried folding chairs in bags over his shoulder and the container of baked beans. They walked along the dock and up to the house.

People filled Old Man Fontenot's front porch and spilled out into the yard on either side.

A small band had set up on a makeshift dais in the grass to the left side of the house. A group of men gathered around a propane-powered burner with a huge pot of seasoned water on top, just beginning to boil. One of the men dumped a bucket of crawfish into the water, the others nodding their approval.

People had brought their own folding chairs, ice chests and beer and were scattered across the front porch and the yard, laughing and talking over the band playing zydeco.

Remy chose a spot on the grass to drop the chairs. Then he and Shelby carried their food offerings to the long tables set up against the house overloaded with everything from fried catfish and hushpuppies to big pots of gumbo.

They found a spot for the cornbread and baked beans.

"Shelby." Gisele appeared from around the corner of the house. "Come wish Old Man Fontenot a happy birthday before he falls asleep in his chair." She grabbed Shelby's hand and led her around the back of the house and up onto the back porch.

A wrinkled old man sat in a rocking chair with a party hat perched on his head, his rheumy eyes staring out at the people milling about his yard. When Gisele and Shelby stopped in front of him, he frowned up at them.

"Happy Birthday, Grandpa Fontenot," Gisele said loud enough to be heard back in town.

Remy remembered visiting Old Man Fontenot when he was a teen. The man had been eighty then.

He was still old but appeared to have shrunk a foot more in twenty years.

He gave Gisele a toothless grin and patted her arm. "Thank you, young lady."

Shelby touched the old man's hand. "Happy Birthday, Grandpa Fontenot."

He looked up at Shelby and thanked her.

The whole scene just reinforced in Remy how beautiful and special Shelby was. She'd worn a pale purple sundress dotted with tiny white roses. She'd pulled her hair up into a loose, messy bun on the crown of her head with tendrils handing down around her ears. She smiled sweetly at the old man and treated him with kindness and respect.

Remy's heart swelled. He was almost jealous of the centenarian.

When the two women came back down the steps, Remy walked up to the old man. "Mr. Fontenot, happy birthday."

The oldest Fontenot stared up at Remy. "Who are you?" he asked in a gravelly voice Remy could barely understand.

Remy leaned close to the old man's ear. "I'm Remy Montagne, sir."

"Montagne," Fontenot said. "The kid that joined the Navy?"

"Yes, sir," Remy responded.

"Home for long?" the old man asked.

"Yes, sir. I'm staying," Remy said.

"Good." The old man pushed his foot against the porch, rocking his chair slightly, ending the conversation.

Remy left the porch, amazed the man remembered that he'd joined the Navy. That had been twenty years ago. He hoped he lived to be that old with all his faculties intact. Smiling, Remy joined Shelby and Gisele.

"You should grab a paper plate and eat," Gisele said. "The mudbugs will be ready in a minute, and there's lots of other good food."

"We will," Shelby smiled. "I'd like to talk to a few folks before I get food stuck between my teeth."

Gisele laughed. "Good point. You should start with Dan. He's the oldest of Fontenot's grandsons and the most responsible." She nodded toward a large man with shaggy black hair and a beer gut, standing with the men tending the crawfish boil.

Shelby nodded. "It's as good a place to start as any other." She took off toward the large man.

Remy hurried after her.

When Shelby stopped beside the man Gisele had indicated, she smiled at him and hugged his neck.

Remy's gut clenched. He didn't like Shelby hugging other men. He'd much prefer she hug him.

Shelby dropped her arms and talked to the man about the weather and the crawfish they were already fishing out of the water.

"Heard you were attacked in the bayou three

nights ago," Dan said with a frown. "Did they catch the guy who did it?"

Shelby shook her head. "No. Were any of your people out on the bayou that night around dusk? Maybe they saw someone out there."

Dan shook his head. "I wasn't out there that night. A couple of my cousins might've been heading in from a bayou tour or chartered fishing gig."

"Do you remember who those cousins were?" Shelby asked. "If they saw anything, it might help me find who hit me. I hate to think someone like that is still out in the bayou. One of your people could be hurt next."

Dan scratched his head for a moment. "Pete Mosier and Ethan Fontenot had charters that day. Talk to them." He frowned. "You might consider staying out of the bayou at night. It ain't safe. Especially for females."

Remy slipped his arm around Shelby. "Thanks for the warning, Dan, but my girl was only doing her job."

Dan's frown deepened. "Not everyone in the bayou is nice. Some people just want to be left alone and are willing to do anything to maintain their privacy."

"The people who attacked me lost their right to privacy when they left me for dead," Shelby said. "It's my responsibility to find them and get them out of the bayou and locked up before they target someone else."

Dan nodded. "Yeah. I get it, but be careful you don't let them finish the job. Now, if you'll excuse me, I have some crawfish to serve up." Dan pushed past Shelby and Remy to help scoop mudbugs and corn cobs from the stock pot onto a large tarp.

Once they'd gotten all the crawfish and corn cobs out of the pot, they gathered the ends of the canvas and carried it to an empty folding table that had been set up next to others full of side dishes.

People grabbed paper plates and loaded food onto them.

Remy and Shelby stood back, observing.

"There's Pete Mosier," Shelby said. "The guy with brown hair scooping potato salad onto his plate right now." She nodded toward another man dipping into an ice chest for a beer. "That's Ethan. Come on."

Remy snagged her arm. "Take it slow. If you ask too many questions, these people will uninvite you from their celebration in a heartbeat. However, if you'd like a beer, I'd gladly get one for you."

"No, thank you, but feel free to help yourself to one," Shelby said. "I think I'll get some potato salad.

"Don't disappear on me," Remy said. "Stay where you can see me, and I can see you."

She nodded. "Got it."

With Shelby in his peripheral vision, Remy

continued to the ice chest where Ethan still stood, tossing back the beer he'd just opened.

"Is this your beer?" Remy asked.

Ethan shook his head. "Anyone can have some. Help yourself."

"Thank you," Remy opened the ice chest, grabbed a beer can and popped the top. "Been a while since I was in town. I'm Remy Montagne." He moved his beer to his left hand and held out his right one to Ethan.

The younger man shook his hand. "Ethan." He lifted his chin toward the house. "The old man is my grandfather."

"Nice party they're throwing for his birthday," Remy said, looking around at everyone who'd come to celebrate.

Ethan shrugged. "If you've got good food, booze and music, folks come."

"I understand the Fontenot family runs a charter boat service." Remy downed a long swallow of beer, his gaze on Shelby striking up a conversation with Pete Mosier.

"Yeah, we do," Ethan said, his foot tapping to the music.

The zydeco band played another song. People gathered in the middle of the yard, dancing to the music.

"How many boats do you operate?"

"We have two airboats and five fishing boats—two

are commercial fishing boats, three are charter fishing boats we use to take tourists out to catch fish in the bayou or out in the Gulf."

"Are you involved in the business?"

He nodded. "I'm a boat captain."

"That must be fun. Beats being stuck behind a desk."

Ethan nodded. "I guess. I couldn't stand being inside all day."

"Which of the boats do you captain?"

"I can handle all of them, but I mainly take people out in the airboat. It handles a lot differently than the fishing boats."

"Nice," Remy said with a grin. "It's been a long time since I've been on an airboat."

"I have a tour going out tomorrow. You can sign up to go with it."

"Thanks. I'll look into it," Remy said. "Do you ever do custom charters?"

"If the price is right," Ethan nodded. "Did one the other day."

"When was that?" Remy asked.

"I don't know," he took a swig of his beer and swallowed. "Maybe three days ago."

Out of the corner of Remy's eye, he spotted Shelby headed his way, leaving Pete Mosier scooping more food onto his plate.

"Good talking to you, Ethan," Remy said. "The

band's playing one of my favorites. Think I'll snag a dance partner and bust some moves."

Remy dropped his beer in a trashcan, hurried toward Shelby, hooked her arm and steered her out into the middle of the yard with the other people dancing.

Shelby frowned. "I'm not very good at dancing."

"You don't have to be; just sway to the beat." Remy lifted her hand, guiding her through a twirl. "See? Easy."

Shelby looked over her shoulder. "I wanted to talk to Ethan."

"I've already talked to him," Remy said. "He was out in an airboat three days ago."

Shelby's eyes widened. "Seriously? Did you ask him whether he saw anyone?"

"He was doing a charter for someone."

"Who?"

"He didn't say."

Her face blanched white. "What if he was the one driving the boat that hit me?" she whispered.

The music slowed to a ballad, giving Remy an excuse to take her into his arms. "He sees us together," Remy said.

"Where is he?" she tried to turn around.

Remy danced her around so that she could look toward Ethan.

"He's heading for the dock," she said. "We should

follow him and ask him if he was the one who hit my boat."

"If he was, do you think he'd admit it?"

She frowned. "Maybe."

"Before we accuse him, we should look at their fleet of boats for damage."

Her frown deepened.

"Where do they dock them?" he asked.

"I don't know," Shelby said. "They come to the marina to pick up customers."

"Who would know where they park their boats otherwise?" he asked.

"Maybe Gisele?" She pulled away from Remy. "I'll ask."

"After the song's over. I like this one." Remy held her close, his cheek resting against her hair.

Her body was stiff. He could tell she wanted to chase after Ethan and demand to know if he was the one who'd tried to kill her. Surrounded by Ethan's family wouldn't be a good time to confront the man.

He moved to the slow, sensuous beat, his hips pressing to hers, his hands resting on the small of her back. "You smell good."

"Mmm, you're not so bad yourself." Shelby relaxed against him, her hands sliding up his chest to lace behind his neck. "We should be asking more questions," she whispered.

"Or dancing," he countered.

"Or dancing," she echoed, her body melting against his.

"Some people say dancing is making love to music," he whispered.

"Better if naked," she murmured.

His dick jerked to attention.

"Ready to leave?" he asked.

She chuckled. "Ready when you are."

"I'm ready now." He stopped just as the music ended.

Remy stepped back and turned toward the dock.

"Oh, there's Gisele," Shelby said. "I'll be right back. I'm going to ask her where the Fontenots keep their boats."

Before he could stop her, Shelby darted after Gisele, leaving him standing alone in the middle of the yard, another sensuous song kicking off.

Hands slid up his back, over his shoulders and down his sides into his pockets, stroking his erection. "Hey, handsome," a woman's voice sounded in his ear.

Not Shelby's.

He stepped forward. The hands in his pockets slipped out.

He spun to face a woman with dark skin, wavy black hair and brown eyes, a smirky smile curving her bright red lips.

Her smile widened slightly, her eyelids drooping. "Where have you been all my life?" She stalked him, closing the short distance between them in two steps. Then she lay her hand on his chest and slid it lower. "Someone got you all hot and bothered?" Her hand shot lower, cupped his package and squeezed.

He jumped back, knocking her hand away. "I don't know who you are, but I'm not interested."

"Too wrapped up trying to get into the pretty deputy's panties to see what you could have instead?" She advanced again, reaching up to curve her hand around his cheek.

"Beat it, Lissette," a different woman's voice sounded from behind Remy. Gisele Gautier stepped up on his left. "He's taken."

"You heard him," Shelby said, coming up on Remy's other side. "He's not interested." She slid her hand into Remy's.

His lips twitched. He turned, tipped Shelby's chin up and brushed his lips across hers. "Hey, beautiful."

Shelby wrapped an arm around his neck and slid her calf up the back of his thigh.

Lissette snorted. "He's not my type anyway."

A moment later, Gisele said, "She's gone."

Maybe she was, but Remy wasn't finished kissing Shelby.

When he finally came up, he stared down into her eyes. "Ready to go?"

"Very," she said, her voice gravelly.

"You don't want to ask anyone else anything? Or

grab something to eat?" he teased, gathering their folding chairs.

"No. We have food at my house." She took his hand and headed for the dock, calling over her shoulder. "Bye, Gisele."

"Bye, Shell," Gisele called out. "Don't forget protection."

Shelby led him to the boat they'd rented from Mitch for the night and waited for him to get in first. Then she untied the line, took his hand and stepped into the boat.

As Shelby settled in the seat beside his, Remy turned the boat around and headed back to the marina. He couldn't get there soon enough. And they still had to drive to her house from there.

Had she put on an act for Lissette? Or did Shelby really want more than just a kiss tonight?

As he maneuvered the boat through the bayou, she reached her hand out and laid it on his thigh, squeezing gently, sending a flash of heat straight to his groin.

Yeah, baby, things just might get hot tonight.

He'd just rounded a bend in the bayou where a cypress tree hung low over the water, blocking his view ahead. As he cleared the low-hanging branches, something flashed in the corner of his eye. On instinct, he jerked the steering wheel to the right.

A boat sped past them, missing them by mere inches, the wake sending their boat rocking violently.

The other boat made a wide circle and came back at them.

Remy slammed the lever forward, giving the 300-horsepower motor full throttle.

"Did you see who was driving?" Remy yelled over the roar of the engine.

"No," she called out, holding on as they whipped around a corner.

With the starlight above and the headlight on the boat, he weaved through the islands and tributaries putting as much distance between him and the other boat.

They made it back to the marina without encountering the other boat again.

Remy grabbed the key from the ignition, helped Shelby out of the boat, secured the craft to the dock and hurried to Shelby's old truck. They were back at her house in record time.

Once they were inside with the door closed and locked behind them, Remy pulled Shelby into his arms and claimed her mouth in a long, hard kiss.

She wrapped her arms around his neck and opened to him, meeting his tongue with hers in a hungry dance.

When he bent to cup her buttocks, she wrapped her legs around his waist. He carried her into her bedroom and kicked the door closed behind him.

"What, not in the daisy room?" she whispered against his mouth.

He growled and dropped her to her feet. "Fuck the daisies." He stood before her, his heart hammering in his chest and every fiber of his being screaming to take her. But he didn't touch her.

Her brow puckered. "What's next?"

"You tell me. Was your act in front of Lissette just an act?"

She shook her head slowly.

"What do you want, Shelby?"

For a moment, she stared at him, her eyes wide, her chest rising and falling as if she'd run a marathon. Then she called out to her smart speaker, "Play some sexy music."

The speaker came on with a soft, sensuous tune.

Shelby moved toward Remy, her hips swaying to the beat. "Some people say dancing is making love to music." Her hand came up to rest against his chest. "I say, making love is dancing to music." She tipped her head back and stared into his eyes. "Let's dance."

CHAPTER 13

SHELBY NEVER CONSIDERED herself a good dancer, but this was different. Remy was different. He made her feel things like she'd never felt before. Every cell in her body burned, sending molten heat to her core.

Dancing with him at the Fontenots had made her forget about chasing down Ethan to get the answers she needed to the question of who had tried to kill her. For the few short minutes the soulful music played, she lost herself in Remy.

Or had she found herself in the arms of a man who had the power to make her aware of her body, her sexuality and her need to be held close?

That need grew like a fanned flame, consuming her in a blast of heat. She tugged his T-shirt out of the waistband of his trousers and dragged it up over his chest, shoulders and head, tossing it aside.

He spun her around and unzipped her dress. His

lips pressed to the back of her neck as he pushed the straps of her dress off her shoulders. The garment floated to the floor.

Shelby stepped free of it, standing there in her best bra, lacy panties and strappy sandals.

She turned to face him and swayed her hips to the music, feeling a little silly until she witnessed the flare in Remy's eyes as his gaze swept her length.

"You're beautiful, Shelby. Inside and out."

She'd never considered herself beautiful, but when Remy said it, she could almost believe him. "Shut up and dance with me," she said.

Remy cupped her face and kissed her gently, then ran his hands down the length of her throat, over her shoulders and down her sides to cup her ass. He brought her closer until the bulge beneath his denim jeans pressed into her belly.

"Do you realize what you do to me?" he growled.

Shelby chuckled. "I do now." She slid her hands into his back pockets and pressed him even closer. "What are we going to do about it?"

"Shut up and dance." Remy found the clasp on her bra and released the hooks, sliding the straps down her arms until the garment dropped to the floor.

She reached for the button at his waistband, thumbed it open and lowered his zipper ever so slowly, savoring the anticipation. "Boxers, briefs or commando?" she murmured.

Three-quarters of the way down the zipper, his cock sprang free into her hands.

She laughed and wrapped her fingers around his length. "Mystery solved."

Remy sucked in a breath. "Geezus, woman. Can we just get naked before I embarrass myself like a teenager with his first orgasm?"

She gave him a sly smile. "I don't know…I think I like you just where I have you."

Remy closed his eyes for a moment and then opened them again. "Two can play that game," he warned.

"Promises. Promises." She ran her finger the length of him, loving how hard he was.

For her.

When the tips of her fingers tapped his balls, he tensed. "Seriously, there's no fun in it for you if I go now."

"That's where you're wrong," she said and dropped to her knees in front of him.

"You shouldn't be straining *yourselfff…*"

Her mouth replaced her fingers. Her teeth gently scraped along his length as she took him all the way in.

He bumped the tip of his dick against the back of her throat and pulled out. Remy paused on the cusp of freeing his cock. "You don't have to do this."

She looked at him as if he'd had a stroke. "Dude,

we're almost naked here. Please tell me you're not going to stop now."

"Oh, hell no," he said. "Unless you say *no*."

"Not happening," Convinced he wasn't going anywhere, she sucked him back in and ran her tongue around him.

When she pushed his hips back out, his fingers twisted into her hair and pulled her to him. In, then out, he thrust. Her hands clutched his ass, making him go harder and faster until he tensed and held steady, his breathing arrested, his cock pulsing.

He gripped her shoulders, lifted her up, scooped her into his arms and laid her on the bed, her feet dangling over the edge in her high heels.

One by one, he removed the shoes and then her panties.

When he came over her, she placed a hand on his chest. "Eh-hem." Her gaze raked over his jean-clad bottom and boots. "Are you getting ahead of yourself?"

He backed up, toed off his boots, shucked his jeans and then crawled onto the bed with her. His body leaned over hers, his erection prodding her belly. "Before we go any further," he said, "let's get one thing straight."

"You already have one thing straight," she said, fondling his stiff shaft.

"Focus, Taylor." He stared down at her, his gaze blazing a path into her soul.

"One thing straight." He lowered his head to steal a kiss before continuing. "This is not a one-night stand."

She frowned up at him, not liking where he was going with this.

"I'm not the kind of man who goes into a relationship for a one-night stand."

"Fine, we can make it two," she said. Then her eyes widened as she remembered. "Wait…what about protection?"

He dove over the side of the bed for his jeans, rummaged in the pocket for his wallet and came up with two condoms and a grin. He set them on the pillow beside her and shook his head. "Not yet."

Shelby frowned. "But—"

"First you."

"I'm already on fire," she said. "I want you inside me. Now."

"Who's in charge here?" he demanded,

"Me," she said, frustration building.

"We'll see," he said with a smirk. He kissed her again and then trailed his lips down the length of her neck and over her collarbone, pausing to suck one of her nipples into his mouth.

Her back arched off the bed, a moan rising in her throat.

He rolled that nipple between his teeth until she writhed beneath him, every nerve cell screaming for more.

Remy switched to the other nipple and flicked and licked it until it pebbled into a tight little nub.

Shelby's hands threaded into his hair, holding him there a moment longer before urging him lower.

With nibbles and licks, he seared a path downward over her ribs, her belly and, finally, to the juncture of her thighs.

"Why are you torturing me?" she moaned.

He laughed. "What? You don't like that? I can stop."

"No!" she cried.

"I want you to come completely apart."

"Confident much?"

"I know what you like." He parted her legs and slipped lower. With his thumbs, he opened her folds and blew a warm stream of air over her clit.

Shelby bucked. Her need for him was almost painful in its intensity. She raised her legs and let them fall to each side, giving him full access to her clit, her pussy...anything he wanted to lick, stroke or fuck. She wanted him so badly she could barely breathe.

He lowered his head and touched his tongue to the most sensitive part of her body.

The electric jolt made her fingers constrict in his hair and her knees pull back.

The second time he touched her there, she cried out. "Again. Please. Again."

He chuckled and applied himself to pleasuring

her, licking, flicking and swirling over her clit until she was wound so tightly, she rocketed over the edge, the sensations shooting through her, spreading to the far corners of her body and soul.

She rode the wave to the very last ripple. As she sank back to the bed, she tightened her hold on Remy's hair and tugged gently.

Shelby grabbed one of the packets, tore it open, rolled it down his shaft and then positioned the tip at her entrance. Her gaze locked with his.

He bent to kiss her long and hard, and then he eased into her, slowly at first.

Shelby gripped his ass and drew him all the way into her.

Her breath caught and held. The man was thick, hard and long. And felt *sooo* good.

He slid out all the way to the tip and then back in.

Shelby closed her eyes and let the wonder of making love for the first time with Remy wash over her like warm water. The sensations seeped into every pore and memory. She'd been thinking about Remy for a very long time.

Caught in the incredible feeling of having Remy thrust in and out of her, Shelby couldn't think past the man and what he was doing to her body.

As he picked up speed, Shelby dug her heels into the mattress. She raised her hips every time he thrust, driving him impossibly deeper.

The longer he pumped, the more his body tensed.

After the most powerful thrust, he buried himself deep inside her, his shaft pulsing against the walls of her slick channel.

His body remained stiff for a long moment as he milked his orgasm to the very last drop.

Then he dropped down on top of Shelby, skin-to-skin, warm and beautiful.

She couldn't breathe and didn't care.

Before she became desperate for air, he rolled to the side and pulled her into his arms.

Shelby rested her head on his arm, sated, fully satisfied and happy. She closed her eyes and revisited the moment in her head, her pussy clenching and unclenching his cock inside.

He'd been so gentle and insistent on pleasing her since this was their first time.

A frown pulled at her forehead. What had he said about this not being a one-night stand? Tonight had been her first time with Remy, and she'd told him she didn't want any strings attached. She always made a point of having no strings attached. She didn't want to end up in the same situation as her mother—married with children one day and divorced and supporting those children the next—no formal education or a skill that would earn enough money to support herself and any kids.

Wait. She hadn't told him the no-strings-attached rule before they'd started. But she felt like she had.

She closed her eyes and thought back through the

night. A different image flashed through her mind—an image of the interior of J.D.'s fishing shack. Only the mattress wasn't folded. It was covered in sheets. Sheets she could feel against her naked skin. And Remy was there as well, naked like he was…now.

Her eyes popped open, and she sat straight up, pulling her pillow over her breasts. She glared down at Remy. "This wasn't our first night together."

He sat up beside her and shook his head. "No, it wasn't." A smile spread across his face. "You remembered."

"Damn right, I did." Anger burned through her. "Why didn't you tell me we'd slept together? The people around me are supposed to fill in the gaps they can. But you didn't. What the hell?"

When he touched her shoulder, she flinched. "Why did you lie to me?"

"I didn't lie," he said softly.

"Withholding the truth is as good as a lie." She threw back the covers and hopped out of bed. Realizing she was fully naked, she grabbed the pillow and paced. "Is that why you said you knew what I wanted?" Shelby didn't wait for an answer. "Don't bother explaining. It's obvious. How else would you know what I like if you hadn't already slept with me? God, I've been so stupid. You must have been laughing your ass off at my expense."

Remy gripped her shoulders lightly. "We'd only been together that one night in the middle of the storm. You insisted on no strings. Not me. I want the strings. But not until you're ready."

"No way. I don't want anything to do with you. And my sister and her husband knew I'd spent the night in the fishing hut with you. They should have at least told me about that. The people I love most didn't fill in the blanks. Why?"

"We thought it would be best for you to remember on your own, especially since it was only one night."

One glorious night making love with Remy.

"That was the night of the tropical storm."

Remy nodded, staring down into her face. "I didn't know how you felt after that night. You were pretty set on a one-night stand with no strings. I had to go back to Montana and couldn't get back for a few weeks." He brushed his lips across her forehead. "I didn't want to force a memory on you that you might not want to hold onto."

Her frown deepened. "It's an excuse."

"It is," he admitted. "And I didn't want to confront you until we could meet in person." His eyes narrowed. "If you remember us, can you remember the people who attacked you?"

Shelby closed her eyes again and thought back to that place in the marsh where she'd been found lying on her overturned boat. All she could see was what she'd seen on her recent visit. No faces surfaced. She opened her eyes, her lips pressing into a thin line. "I can't remember anything to do with the attack."

"Don't worry," he said and pulled her into his arms.

Shelby wanted to stay mad at him for not telling her about their connection and making love. But she couldn't when he held her in his arms.

"I'm sorry, Shelby." He stroked his hand down her back. "I wanted you to want to be with me for me. Not for a memory you couldn't quite remember.

She leaned her forehead against his chest. "I want to be mad at you."

He chuckled. "But you can't because I make you laugh."

"And you protect me." She curled her fingers into his shirt. "Promise me you won't keep information from me again."

"Deal," he said and swept her up into his arms to carry her back to the bed, where he held her in his arms.

"Remy?" She trailed her fingers across his chest.

"Yes?"

"Would you have come back to Bayou Mambaloa if my sister hadn't called you?" Shelby asked.

"Absolutely. I wanted to stay when I was here last, but I had a job to go to. I wasn't sure how I'd come home again. Fortunately, Hank had it in mind to set up the Bayou Brotherhood Protectors and wanted me to do it." Remy smiled. "He didn't have to ask me twice. I was coming home even if I had to quit and find some other job."

"I'm glad you came home," Shelby whispered as she closed her eyes and snuggled against him.

"What about your no-strings rule?" Remy asked.

She sighed. "I might have to revisit that rule. For tonight, I don't have the energy or inclination to think about it."

"Sleep, sweetheart," he said. "We can conquer the world tomorrow."

"That's right. We have to find the boat that rammed mine. If it is the one Ethan had that evening, then we can bring him in for questioning and find out who he's working with." Shelby yawned. "I'm ready to be done with this. I don't much like being a target."

"I don't like that you're a target either. The boat that almost hit us tonight came too close for my comfort."

"Mine, too." She laid her hand on his chest. "We should get those deadbolts installed tomorrow."

"We will," he said.

Beyond tired, Shelby slipped into a deep sleep. Tomorrow they'd find who was responsible for the troubles and end this nightmare.

CHAPTER 14

THE FOLLOWING DAY, Remy was up before Shelby, had breakfast made and coffee brewing by the time she stumbled out of the bedroom and into the kitchen, wrapped in a bathrobe and nothing else.

She walked into his arms and leaned her cheek against his naked chest. "I like it when you cook in jeans and nothing else."

"I like this robe. But you know what I like better? When you wear nothing at all." He untied the sash and slipped his hands beneath to touch her skin and feather his fingers around her waist to cup her ass.

He lifted her onto the kitchen table and stepped between her legs.

She reached for the button on his jeans, released it and rode the zipper down with her fingers.

It didn't take much to get Remy hard when it

came to Shelby's body and her hands... Oh, those hands.

She worked his cock until it was so hard he could hammer nails. She reached into the robe pocket, pulled out a condom and smiled. "Whatcha got cooking?"

"You, baby." When he reached for the packet, she pulled it away.

"No, really. Whatcha got cooking?"

He glanced over her shoulder to the stove. "Nothing. I just finished frying the bacon. The burners are off."

"In that case..." She tore open the packet and rolled the condom over his engorged staff. "I've never done it on a table."

"We need to remedy that lack of experience," he said as he cupped her sex with his hand and slid a finger into her already damp entrance. "What's this?" he said, swirling his fingers around.

"I was thinking of you." She gripped his cock. "I see you were thinking of me."

"It's hard not to." Using her juices as a lubricant, he touched her clit with the tip of his finger, then swirled it around, pinching it lightly.

Shelby squirmed on the table. The more he played with her clit, the more she rocked and moaned.

"Now, Remy," she said, her voice breathy.

He stepped up to the table, scooted her bottom to the edge and touched his dick to her wet center.

Then he slid into her, not stopping until he was seated all the way to the hilt.

Then, holding her hips, he rocked into her, increasing his speed with each thrust until he had her and the table rocking.

Moments later, he shot over the top, his orgasm intense, his cock throbbing against her channel.

Shelby wrapped her legs around his waist and held him inside her as long as she could, her head thrown back, riding her own orgasm.

When they finally came back to earth and the kitchen, he lifted her from the table and carried her into the bathroom.

They showered together, rubbing soap over every inch of each other's bodies.

Remy loved touching Shelby. "You're beautiful," he said as he dried her breasts, waist and hips.

After they dressed, they ate sandwiches, then drove to the hardware store and bought two deadbolt locks and a security system Remy would help her install.

They dropped the purchases in the old truck and drove to Gisele's store on Main Street, The Mamba Wamba Art and Gifts.

Gisele met them at the door and invited them in. Her dark hair was pulled back in a tight bun, emphasizing her high, dark cheekbones and luminous brown eyes. "I take it you two finally had sex," she said with a broad grin. "About time."

Though heat rose in Remy's cheeks, he didn't confirm or deny having sex with Shelby.

Shelby, on the other hand, gripped Gisele's arm. "I remembered Remy's and my first time in the bayou at J.D.'s fishing hut."

Gisele nodded. "So, you did have sex." Her eyebrow rose. "But in J.D.'s old shack?"

Shelby shook her head. "The fish hut was during the storm a few weeks ago. The last time Remy was in town was our first time together. I remembered."

Gisele hugged her. "That's good, right? Were you able to remember who tried to kill you?"

Shelby's shoulders sank. "Sadly, no. But I hope this means it'll come back soon. I hate walking around not knowing who has it out for me."

"I know, honey," Gisele patted her arm. "But you have this hunky fella looking out for you. It can't be all bad."

Shelby smiled up at Remy. "It's not. Having Remy around has its…perks."

Remy's heart swelled at the smile Shelby directed toward him. He touched a hand to the small of her back, wishing they could go back to her house and spend the day in bed together. But as long as she was in danger, they couldn't wallow in bed making mad passionate love.

"What brings you to Mamba Wamba so early?" Gisele asked.

"We hope you can help us find the boat that ran over mine," Shelby said.

"If I knew which one had done it, don't you think I would've told you by now?" Gisele touched her arm. "You're my dearest friend."

Shelby hugged her. "We think Ethan Fontenot might have been driving the boat that rammed mine. "

"Ethan?" Gisele's brow puckered. "He's not the kind of guy who'd ram another craft with one of the family's fleet boats."

"We spoke with Ray Fontenot, his supervisor," Remy said. "Ethan and Pete had boats out late that afternoon when Shelby was attacked.

"I spoke with Peter," Shelby said. "He had a family of six on his fishing boat, aged seven to sixty-six years old. They had some engine trouble on their way back to the marina that kept them out later than scheduled. We'll touch bases with Mitch at the marina, but I don't think Pete's our guy."

"And I had a chat with Ethan," Remy said. "He told me he'd had a charter that day with the airboat. We need to find that airboat and see if it's as scraped and banged up as Shelby's boat."

Gisele nodded. "I just find it hard to believe Ethan would do that. But then, he's been actin' weird lately. He's been hangin' around my cousin Lissette too much. She's a bad influence."

"Any idea where we'd find Ethan's airboat?" Shelby asked.

"If it's not at the marina, it will be parked close to the house of one of them who drives it," Gisele said. "Ethan rents a two-bedroom shack on the bayou south of town. Lissette lives in a garage apartment not far from him. There's a community dock that residents of the neighborhood can use to tie up their boats. I've seen an airboat there recently. Can't imagine it belongs to anyone else."

"We'll check it out," Remy said. "The others?"

Gisele shrugged. "The commercial boats are located on the bayou beside Dan Fontenot's home. He has his own dock. The fishing boats are located at Marceau's Marina. Simon might take the bass boat home since it's faster to go across the water than it is to cut a path across the land."

"Thanks, Gisele," Shelby said. "We'll check them out, starting with the airboat near Ethan's place."

"Good luck finding the boat." Gisele hugged Shelby.

They left the Mambo Wambo gift shop and stepped out on the sidewalk.

A door opened several buildings down from the gift shop, and a dark-haired man dressed in a business suit emerged, followed by LaShawnda Jones, wearing a periwinkle skirt suit with a long, slim skirt. She gave the man a tight smile, shook his hand and turned to go back inside her office. When she spotted Remy and Shelby, she hesitated, her gaze shifting to the gentleman walking away from her.

The man in the suit strode toward a Porsche sports car. As he opened the car door, his head turned toward Remy and Shelby, and his eyes narrowed.

"I wonder who he is," Shelby murmured beside Remy.

The man got into his sports car and drove away.

Moments later, LaShawnda hurried toward Remy and Shelby. "That was awkward," the woman said with a laugh. "The man who just left was your competition for the boat factory."

"He didn't look happy," Shelby said. "Who is he? I haven't seen him around town."

"Thomas Sanders. He's from Atlanta. He's looking to invest in a manufacturing facility." LaShawnda shrugged. "If he had a problem about losing the bid, he should've taken it out on his own agent." She shook off her frown and smiled. "I'm so glad to catch you this morning."

Shelby smiled at the woman. "Good to see you, LaLa."

"Shelby, Remy," LaShawnda nodded to each before directing her attention at Remy. "I got news this morning that the bank accepted your offer on the boat factory. They want to close as soon as possible. I also heard from the owner of the boarding house. He also accepted your offer." She held out her hand to Remy. "Congratulations, Remy."

Shelby touched his arm, a smile spreading across her face. "That's great news."

"Thank you." Remy shook LaShawnda's hand, relieved one more thing was going right with his move home. Between Shelby remembering their night in the fishing hut and nailing the purchase of the buildings they'd need for the new branch of the Brotherhood Protectors, things were looking up.

"Thank you for letting me represent you in your purchases," LaShawnda said with a smile, her hand still in Remy's. "I'll stop by Shelby's house later this evening to drop off a little gift to show my appreciation."

"Well, aren't we all having a little celebration here," a female voice said behind Remy.

Remy and Shelby turned to find Lissette standing behind them, wearing a flowing dress in varying shades of bright orange, a chunky gold necklace and an array of gold bangles around her wrists. She looked the part of a beautiful Voodoo priestess with her hair woven in slender braids, hanging down to the middle of her back.

She laid a manicured hand on his arm and smiled up at him. "To what do we owe the occasion?" Her tone was more of a feline purr as she batted false eyelashes up at him.

No one spoke.

Lissette's eyes narrowed. "Well, if our lovely realtor is any indication, she's just made a sale, and our returning hero is the buyer." She held out a slim dark hand to Remy. "Congratulations, Remy, darling."

He didn't want to touch the woman, but Remy figured it would be rude if he ignored her outstretched hand. He shook the hand. "Thank you." He tried to pull free of her grip.

Lissette didn't let go. "What did you buy? A house to set down roots and have a family? What do you want? Two, maybe three little curtain climbers?" Her free hand swept over his shoulder and down his arm. "I can help you with that."

Using his other hand, Remy peeled her fingers from around his and stepped back. "No house. No babies for now, and no thank you for your offer to help."

Shelby moved forward and hooked her arm through Remy's elbow. "Remy's already got a woman in his life."

Delighted that Shelby had stepped in, Remy slid his arm around Shelby's waist and smiled down at her. "That's right. I already have a woman. A beautiful one at that."

"Hmmph." Lissette tossed her long braids over her shoulder. "If you like boring women who know only one position. I, on the other hand, would make your life exciting and positively unforgettable."

Shelby's lips pressed together.

Remy's arm tightened around Shelby's waist. "I've lived exciting and unforgettable, some of which I wish I could forget. It's exhausting. I want real and lasting with memories that make me smile. I want a life with a woman who makes my heart race and my breath catch when I see her standing across a room." He looked down into Shelby's eyes. "I have everything I want and need."

Lissette lifted her chin and stared down her nose. "Good luck with that. Not everything turns out as you expect." She turned and entered Gisele's store.

LaShawnda stared at the door Lissette had disappeared through. "That girl needs a come-to-Jesus reset." She faced Remy and Shelby. "Thanks again. I hope you have a beautiful day." The realtor spun on her stiletto heels and returned to her office.

Shelby sighed. "Lissette's drama exhausts me. Shall we get on with our investigation?"

"Yes, ma'am." He pulled out his phone. "Let me make a call first." He called Hank.

Hank answered on the first ring. "Montagne, how's Miss Taylor?"

"Better. She's starting to remember but hasn't been able to remember the incident that landed her in the hospital."

"The sheriff's department have any leads?"

"Not yet. I need you to have Swede do a background check on a few people."

"Who've you got?" Hank asked.

"Ethan and Simon Fontenot, Lissette Gautier and Thomas Sanders."

"On it," Hank said. "Anything else?"

He told Hank about the near miss in the bayou.

"So, she's still being targeted," Hank said. "I'm glad you're there. The guys left yesterday in a caravan of trucks and SUVs."

"Which brings me to a bit of good news," Remy said.

Hank chuckled. "Always appreciate good news."

"The bank accepted the offer on the boat factory and the owner selling the boarding house agreed to our offer as well."

"That is good news. I'll have Swede check into contractors. You focus on resolving Miss Taylor's situation. Swede will get back to you as soon as he has a chance to look into those names. He's still working on getting more information from the DEA about the Colombian Cartel. He's trying to get pictures of prominent individuals who've been spotted in the US recently."

"Anything he can come up with could help," Remy said. "In the meantime, we'll look for the boat that rammed Shelby's."

"That could be like looking for a needle in a haystack where you are," Hank said.

"We have to start somewhere," Remy glanced at

Shelby. "A boat doesn't come out unscathed when ramming another."

"True," Hank said. "Good luck."

Remy ended the call and looked at Shelby. "Let's go."

She led the way to the truck, slid into the passenger seat and waited for Remy to climb in behind the steering wheel. "It might be faster to do our looking around by boat."

"Agreed." Remy aimed for the marina.

Marceau had a bass boat available. After he gassed it up, they left the marina and headed straight for Ethan's place. The community dock had an assortment of boats, none of which were Fontenot's air or bass boats.

"If not here, where would Ethan leave his airboat?" Remy mused. "Should we check out Dan and Simon's places?"

"If Ethan's airboat was the one that rammed me, would he moor it where anyone could see it?" Shelby looked around. "Maybe we should look in some of the coves close by."

Remy steered the boat away from the dock and followed the shoreline into the nearest cove. It was empty, as well as the next three coves.

Remy turned the boat around, heading for Dan Fontenot's place. "That boat has to have some damage from ramming yours. Could it be in a shop being repaired?"

"That's a distinct possibility. The nearest boat repair shops are in Thibodaux." Shelby pulled out her cell phone, looked up the numbers and called the first one. Shelby pressed the phone to her ear and waited.

A couple of moments later, she said, "This is Deputy Taylor from Bayou Mambaloa. Have you had an airboat brought in the past three days for repairs to the front end and hull?" She nodded. "I'll wait."

Remy picked up the pace, arriving at Dan Fontenot's place while Shelby was still on hold.

Only one boat was tied to the dock, a small jon boat with a thirty-horsepower motor.

"No? Thank you for checking." She ended the call, tried the next one with the same request and waited for the customer representative to get back to her.

Remy moved on to Simon Fontenot's place. The little cottage perched on the edge of the bayou had a small dock with nothing tied to it.

"You did? Could you give me that boat's vehicle identification and registration numbers?" She put the cell phone on speaker and brought up a notes application. As the customer service representative fed her the VIN and registration numbers, Shelby keyed them into her notes.

While Shelby placed a call to the state department of motor vehicles, Remy headed back to Marceau's Marina.

He was pulling up to the dock when Shelby ended the call and looked toward him. "The airboat at

Bordeaux's Best Boat Repairs is registered to Fontenot's Fishing and Bayou Tours."

"Just need to get to the boat repair shop and check out the damage." Remy helped her out of the boat. They returned the keys to Mitch and hurried to Shelby's truck.

"I'm going to give Sheriff Bergeron a heads up. He needs to be ready to bring Ethan in if we find the damage commensurate to what happened to my boat."

"Aren't you afraid he'll put the kibosh on your investigation?" Remy asked.

Shelby frowned. "You're right. I'll wait until we have proof."

Thirty minutes later, they arrived at the boat repair shop.

Shelby flashed her badge and asked to see the airboat belonging to the Fontenots.

The man at the desk escorted them to where the boat was parked on a trailer in the back parking lot.

One look and Remy knew. "This has to be the boat that hit you."

Shelby closed her eyes.

"Are you okay?" Remy rested a hand on the small of her back.

She nodded. "I had a flash of memory."

He waited for her to reveal what she'd remembered.

When she opened her eyes, she gave him a twisted

grin. "I can't force those memories out. The harder I try, the more elusive they are." She clenched her fist, a fierce frown denting her forehead. "But there was a memory. An image of a boat coming right at me."

"This one?" Remy asked.

"It happened so fast, and the memory is vague." She shook her head. "It could have been."

Shelby snapped photos of the airboat from all angles and took a photo of the VIN. She turned to the service attendant. "Don't do anything with this boat until someone from the sheriff's department gets back to you."

"Yes, ma'am," the attendant said.

Shelby pulled out her cell phone, called Sheriff Bergeron and hit the speaker button. "I think we found the boat that hit mine. It's here at Bordeaux's Best Boat Repairs in Thibodaux. Ethan Fontenot had a charter in that boat the evening I was attacked."

"I should be mad at you for conducting an investigation while you're officially on medical leave," the sheriff said. "But I'm so short-handed, I've barely had time to think. I'll get a tow truck over there to take it to the impound lot until the state crime lab can process it. And I'll go personally to bring Ethan Fontenot in." He chuckled. "Personally, because everyone else is tied up. Hurry up and get well. We need you back at work. And please tell me you didn't drive yourself to Thibodaux."

"No, sir," Remy said. "This is Remy Montagne. I'm

her chauffeur until she gets clearance from her doctor."

"Good. Hey, Montagne, are you looking for work in the area? I could use another deputy."

Remy smiled at Shelby. "Thank you, Sheriff Bergeron, but I've already got a job. Besides, you have one of the best coming back to work soon."

"Damn right, I do. Deputy Taylor is top-notch. I don't know what I'd do without her." He snorted. "Well, I do know now, and I hope it doesn't last long. I'll get on it. You get back to recovering."

"Yes, sir," Shelby said and ended the call.

They stayed until the tow truck arrived to collect the boat. The sun was setting by the time they got on the road back to Bayou Mambaloa.

Shelby leaned back her head and closed her eyes. "I want to be relieved that Ethan is being brought in for questioning, but I know it's just the beginning. He's not smart enough to conduct a drug trafficking operation by himself."

"Hopefully, he can shed some light on who's in charge," Remy said.

Shelby's cell phone chirped. She glanced down at the caller ID and hit the receive button. "Sheriff Bergeron."

As she listened, her face lost all color. "I understand. Yes, sir, I'll be careful." She ended the call and stared out the front windshield as if in shock. "Well, damn."

Remy shot a glance at Shelby. "What?"

Her lips were thin, and her jaw tight. "The sheriff went to Ethan's home. No one answered. He checked the door. It was unlocked, so he went inside." Her gaze met Remy's. "He found Ethan."

Remy knew before she said the words.

"He was lying on the living room floor, hands tied behind his back." Shelby's voice cracked. "He had a plastic bag wrapped around his head and an X painted across his chest. Dead."

CHAPTER 15

"Do you have any woodworking tools, drills or power tools at your house?" Remy asked as they drove into Bayou Mambaloa.

Shelby shook her head. "I have some basic tools like a couple of screwdrivers and an adjustable wrench. Anything else, I borrow from Alan. He's got every power tool known to man in the shop behind his house."

"Will anyone be home?" he asked.

Shelby called Chrissy, who assured her she was home, cooking dinner for the kids, Alan and Gerard, and they were welcome to borrow any tool they needed.

Remy drove straight to Alan and Chrissy's house.

Chrissy met Shelby at the door with a hug and a worried frown. "I heard about Ethan. Frankly, I'm terrified. You should come stay with us."

Shelby shook her head. "I can't. I shouldn't be here now, but we need tools to install deadbolts on my doors."

"By all means, help yourself to whatever you need in Alan's shop," she said, waving toward the rear of the house. "And grab Gerard. He's in the living room with the kids. He might want a break from them."

Shelby helped her sister butter garlic bread while Remy went through the shop behind the house, gathering the tools he'd need to install the deadbolts in Shelby's home.

Chrissy pulled a lasagna out of the oven and set it on a trivet. "So, other than living in terror, how's it going? Have any of your memories returned?"

Shelby nodded. "I remembered staying in J.D.'s fishing hut."

Chrissy's eyes lit up. "You remembered the storm and Remy finding you when your boat motor quit working?"

"I did," Shelby said. "Everything about that night with Remy."

"You never told me exactly what happened between you and Remy during that storm, but I bet Alan a hundred dollars you two did it."

"Chrissy!" Shelby's hand stopped in mid-smear over a piece of garlic bread.

"It's not like we're children, or I'm your mother. You're a grown woman with needs and desires. Remy's a good-looking guy. You've had a crush on him since forever. It adds up. One plus one makes whoopee." She grinned. "And what triggered the memory?" She raised her hand. "No, let me guess… you remembered in the middle of making love."

Heat flooded Shelby's cheeks.

Chrissy clapped her hands. "Mama's buying a new purse. Alan is convinced nothing happened between you two." She hugged Shelby. "I'm so happy for you. Remy's a good man."

"Just because we've had sex twice doesn't mean we're halfway down the aisle to wedded bliss."

"No?" Chrissy raised an eyebrow. "I predict it will happen within the next year. No, make that six months. You two aren't getting any younger. You'll have to start popping out babies right away before your eggs all shrivel up."

Remy chose that moment to come through the back door with Gerard, both carrying a box full of tools.

Shelby's cheeks burned with embarrassment.

Remy frowned. "Are you all right?"

"She's fine," Chrissy said. "Healthy as a broodmare."

Shelby swatted her sister. "Ignore her. My sister has lost her mind." She laid the last slice of garlic bread in a basket, covered it with a cloth and wiped her hands on a paper towel. "Got everything we'll need?"

He nodded.

"You two should stay for dinner," Chrissy said. "I made plenty."

"Thanks," Remy said, "but we'll pass. I want to get these deadbolts installed before dark."

Chrissy smiled. "Understood. We'll have more opportunities in the future to have you over for dinner. Stay safe."

Gerard and Remy carried the boxes out to the truck.

"Tell Alan thanks for the use of his tools," Shelby said. "We'll get them back to him as soon as possible."

"No worries." Chrissy hugged her. "Please be safe. I love you so much and look forward to our children growing up together."

"Seriously, Chris, don't count the chickens yet." She kissed her sister's cheek. "I love you, too." Shelby hurried outside and climbed into the truck.

Remy's cell phone rang. He pulled it from his pocket and answered the call. "Hey, Hank, hold on, I'm putting you on speaker. I'm here with Shelby."

"Remy, it's Swede. I'm just following up on the people whose names you gave to Hank."

"What did you find?"

"Simon Fontenot, nothing more than a speeding ticket. Ethan Fontenot has a couple of speeding tickets and a record of indebtedness. He had a vehicle repossessed and has been turned over to a collection agency for thirty-five thousand dollars of credit card debt. He's behind on his rent, and the landlord has filed an eviction notice."

"The sheriff found Ethan dead in his house today," Remy said.

"Suicide?" Swede asked.

"No," Remy said. "Murder."

"Loan shark collecting on his debt?" Swede asked.

Remy described how Ethan had been found.

Swede let out a low whistle. "Sounds more like something the Equis Cartel would do. That's one of their preferred methods of execution."

Shelby's chest tightened, and her pulse pounded. "Evidence they are, in fact, here in Bayou Mambaloa?" she whispered.

"Sounds like it," Swede said. "Lissette Gautier has been arrested several times with all charges dropped. She's had some recent large deposits made to her bank account from an account I'm still trying to trace. I stall out in the Cayman Islands."

"Do you think she might be working with the Colombian Cartel?" Remy asked.

"I wouldn't put it past her," Shelby said.

"We can't say for sure, but large deposits like that are usually linked to illegal activities."

"What about Thomas Sanders?" Remy asked.

"We didn't find much on him. We traced his vehicle

registration to an address in Atlanta. But that's all we found. No record of employment or anything else. His bank account hasn't had any deposits or withdrawals in months. If he's using credit cards, they aren't in his name. The Porsche he's driving was a cash purchase. I'm compiling a list of cartel members and their photos. I'll send it over as soon as I get a couple more. That way, you can keep your eyes open in case one of them shows up in Bayou Mambaloa. That's all I have for now."

"Thanks, Swede," Remy said and ended the call.

"Interesting about Ethan and Lissette," Shelby said.

"Yeah, but it doesn't make me feel any better. Let's get to your place and install these locks."

A few minutes later, they were at Shelby's house. They spent the next two hours installing the deadbolts and the new doorknobs. Shelby worked alongside Remy, removing old doorknobs, handing him tools and tightening screws.

When they finished, Remy handed her the key. "This is the real test. See if it works."

Shelby inserted the key into the pretty new lock and twisted it. The lock opened. She tried the same key in the doorknob lock. It opened.

With a grin, she gave Remy a high-five. "Good job, team."

He swung her up in his arms and carried her across the threshold. Once inside, he kissed her, set her on her feet and turned to lock the deadbolt and the doorknob.

He gave her a stern look. "No more leaving a key outside."

Shelby gave him a saucy salute. "Yes, sir. And thank you." She leaned up on her toes and kissed him. "I had fun and learned a thing or two."

He pulled her into his arms. "Oh, yeah? What did you learn?" He pressed his lips to her forehead.

"How to install a deadbolt for one." She slid her hands around the back of his neck. "And that I could get used to having you around."

His lips twisted in a wry grin. "I'm good for fixing things, huh?"

She nodded. "Yup."

"Is that all I'm good for?" He kissed the tip of her nose.

She tilted her head as if thinking about his question. "You're good for other things."

His mouth moved to her neck, where he kissed just below her ear. "Like?"

He was doing crazy things to her, making her blood burn through her veins. "Like that."

Remy pulled her shirt over her head and tossed it onto a chair. He unclipped her bra and lowered his head to take one of her nipples into his mouth, sucking hard.

"And that," she breathed, clasping her hands behind his head. "Definitely that."

He chuckled, his hands moving to release the button on her jeans and lower her zipper. Sliding his hand into her panties, he cupped her sex and slipped a finger into her warm wetness.

Her head dropped back, a moan rising in her throat. "And that."

She reached for his shirt, ripping it out of his waistband, her movements jerky, born of a desperation to be naked with him.

He took over, yanked his shirt over his head and shucked his jeans.

Shelby shimmied out of her jeans and panties and kicked them to the side. Then she took his hand and led him to her bedroom, where they fell into bed and made love so tenderly. Shelby's heart swelled with emotion.

When they lay spent in each other's arms, Shelby sighed. "Like that." Her stomach rumbled.

"Hungry?" Remy asked.

"I am," she said, not making a move to get up.

"I'm going to get a shower, then I'll cook something for dinner." Remy leaned over her and kissed her. "You could join me."

"I could if I had any bones left in my body. I think they've all melted." She smiled up at him. "You do that to me."

"Mmm..." He kissed her again. "I'm good like that."

"Yes, you are." She cupped the back of his neck

and pulled him back down for another kiss. "Get the water warm, and I'll join you."

"Deal." He rolled off the bed onto his feet and headed for the bathroom.

Shelby's gaze followed his sexy, naked butt.

"I could get used to this," she murmured.

"Did you say something?" Remy called out from the bathroom as he turned on the water.

"Is it warm yet?" she answered.

Shelby heard the ping of a text message received on her cell phone in the other room. She rose, wrapped a robe around her body and walked into the living room where she'd left her cell phone.

LaShawnda had sent a message to her and Remy.

Left a gift basket on your porch. Don't leave it outside long. Some of it is edible. Thank you for your business.

CURIOUS, Shelby crossed to the front door, twisted the knob and pulled before she remembered she had to unlock the deadbolt as well.

She twisted the lever, smiling as she did, thinking, *Nothing says love like installing a deadbolt.*

Did Remy love her? Or was he just doing his job as a protector?

Shelby was almost certain it was too soon to know, at least on his part. She'd always loved Remy.

First, as a childhood crush. Now, she loved him with all her heart and soul.

He might take a little longer to come to the same conclusion. She was willing to wait.

Shelby pulled open the door and frowned.

Lissette stood there with a basket in her arms, wearing the same orange outfit from earlier. "Hey, Shelly, I found this on your porch and thought you might want me to take it inside."

"What are you doing here?" Shelby demanded.

"Just wanted to pay my favorite deputy a visit. Is there any law against that?" She stepped forward. "Aren't you going to invite me in?"

Shelby planted herself in Lissette's way. "No. I'm not going to invite you in. Give me the basket and go home." When she reached for the basket, Lissette pulled it away.

"I really need to talk to you," Lissette said, her brow furrowing.

"We have nothing to talk about," Shelby said. "Give me the basket and go home."

Still holding the basket out of Shelby's reach, Lissette said, "I need to talk to you about Ethan."

Shelby's eyes narrowed. "What about Ethan?" Did she know he was dead?

Of course, she knew. It was a small town. Everyone knew.

Lisette knotted. "He wasn't the one driving the

boat that rammed yours. Let me in, and I'll tell you everything."

Shelby hesitated. She didn't trust Lissette, but did she know something about the attack? Ethan couldn't confess now that he was dead.

"Shelby?" Remy called out.

Shelby glanced over her shoulder.

In that one second she turned away from Lissette, the door she held onto exploded inward, sending Shelby stumbling backward.

Before she could right herself, she was caught by a man dressed entirely in black, wearing a black ski mask over his face. He spun her around, clamped an arm around her neck and pressed cold, hard metal against her temple.

If she fought to breathe, would he pull the trigger? Either way, she'd die.

"Shelby?" Remy's voice called out. "What the hell was that—" He emerged from the hallway with a bath towel wrapped around his hips and a gun in his hand. He ground to a halt when he saw Shelby.

"Drop the gun," said the man holding her.

Shelby didn't recognize the voice.

"Do it, Remy," Lissette said from behind Shelby and the man whose arm was cutting off her air.

"Don't hurt her," Remy said.

"I won't if you drop the gun," the man said.

"How do I know you won't hurt her?" Remy said,

the gun still in his hand, aimed at Shelby and the stranger.

"You don't, but if you don't, I'll pull the trigger on your girlfriend. Your choice."

"Do it, Remy," Lissette urged. "Thomas isn't kidding. He'll put a bullet in her."

"Shut up," the man said.

"I'm only trying to help," Lissette whined.

"I said shut up!" The man pressed the gun into Shelby's temple harder. "Drop the damn gun."

"Take it easy. I'll put it down. Just don't hurt her." Remy bent to lay the gun on the ground.

"Don't do it," Shelby wheezed. "He'll kill us anyway." Her captor tightened his hold around her neck.

"Maybe he won't," Remy said. "I think Mr. Sanders is a reasonable man. We just need to know what he wants."

Shelby had to do something soon or die. And she couldn't die. She had to stay alive long enough to make sure Remy wasn't killed. The thought of Remy dying in the same manner Ethan had been killed turned her stomach.

Remy laid the gun at his feet.

As he straightened, his gaze locked with Shelby's.

She blinked several times, hoping he'd take it as a signal that she was about to do something.

Lissette laughed. "You're as stupid as Ethan. Do you want me to tie them up?"

"Shut up, Lissette," the man said.

"Just so you know..." Lissette stood next to Shelby, a sneer pulling her lip up one side. "I rammed your shitty little boat. Ethan didn't have the balls. You were supposed to be dead."

"And you screwed that up," the man in black said.

"But we have them now. All you have to do is kill them, and no one will be the wiser. Your boss will still be the fine, upstanding citizen coming to town to start a business that will employ locals and run his product on the side.

"You talk too damn much. I ought to kill you, too."

"I'm shutting up," Lissette said. "But you didn't answer me." She held up zip ties. "Want me to tie them up?"

He nodded. "Do it."

Shelby blinked three times at Remy and went limp.

The man holding her struggled to maintain his hold for a few seconds, then gave up and let her fall to the floor.

He straightened and raised his weapon, aiming at Remy.

Remy yanked his towel off and whipped it toward the man's gun as he pulled the trigger.

Remy kicked the gun toward Shelby and dove at the intruder, plowing into him like a charging bull.

Shelby scrambled on her hands and knees, reaching for the gun.

Once she had the gun in her hand, she rolled to her feet and aimed it at the two men battling to control the intruder's weapon.

An ear-splitting shriek sounded from behind Shelby. Lissette pounced on Shelby's back and wrapped an arm around her neck. "No fucking way. You were supposed to die in your shitty boat." She pounded her fist on Shelby's head.

Shelby grabbed the arm around her neck and flipped the woman over her head.

Lissette landed on her back and, like a cat, was immediately back on her feet, charging toward Shelby.

Shelby shifted the gun in her hand, waited until the last second, then stepped to the left and slammed the butt of the handgun into the side of Lissette's head, sending the other woman crashing into the wall.

Lissette slid to the floor and lay still.

Shelby looked from Lissette to the fighting men and back. She grabbed one of the zip ties Lissette had brandished, quickly secured the woman's wrists behind her back and applied another to her ankles.

Then Shelby spun to help Remy with the man in black.

His ski mask had come off. The man fighting Remy for control of the gun was not Thomas Sanders, the man competing to purchase the boat factory. She didn't recognize the man and didn't care. He couldn't win this fight.

She held the gun steady and waited for her chance.

The two men fell to the floor. Remy held the man's wrist, pointing the gun away from them.

The man in black bucked and rolled.

Remy held on and rolled with him.

Shelby couldn't get a clear shot. The men rolled again.

The intruder was on top this time.

Shelby aimed at his back but didn't fire. If she did, the bullet could go through both men. She couldn't risk it.

A shot rang out.

Shelby froze.

The men lay still, the struggle over.

Shelby ran toward them. "Remy? Oh, dear God. Remy!"

"Help me," he said from beneath the other man.

Her heart in her throat, Shelby dropped the gun, grabbed one arm of the man in black and tugged as hard as she could, dragging him over until he rolled onto his back.

Remy lay on his back, blood staining his naked chest.

"You're hurt!" Shelby dropped to her knees and felt around his chest for the wound, tears filling her eyes, blurring her vision. "Geezus! Where's the damned wound?"

He caught her hand in his. "Shelby, sweetheart. It's not my blood."

She leaned back and blinked away the tears. "You're not hurt?"

He sat up. "No."

Shelby flung herself into his arms. "I almost lost you. Damn you. I almost lost you."

"But you didn't. And the best part is that you're okay. I thought he'd kill you before I had a chance to tell you..."

"When I heard that shot…I thought…I thought you were dead." She stared up into his eyes.

He smoothed her hair back from her damp face.

She shook her head. "I was afraid you were dead, and I didn't get the chance to tell you…"

"I love you," he said.

"Yes. That." She smiled. "I love you. I always have."

"No," he said. "That's not what I meant."

She frowned. Confused. "But I do. I love you."

He chuckled. "Listen to what I said."

Shelby's frown deepened. "I'm listening."

Remy pointed to himself. "I. Love. You." He pointed to her.

As understanding dawned, Shelby's heart exploded with emotion. Still, she hesitated.

"Seriously?" She shook her head. "Isn't it too soon? I mean, I've known all my life that I loved you."

He kissed her lips gently. "And I've known for exactly three weeks, five days and twelve hours. I have a lot of time to make up."

"You can start now."

Remy laughed and pulled her into his arms. "I love you, Deputy Taylor."

Shelby wrapped her arms around the man she loved with all her heart and held on tight.

EPILOGUE

ONE MONTH LATER...

REMY STOOD inside the Bayou Boat Factory building, looking around at what they'd accomplished in one month's time with ten hard-working men, elbow grease and several giant roll-off trash bins full of junk hauled off to the recycle center and dump.

Most of the equipment left behind over the years had been inoperative and could only be salvaged for the metal.

By the time the sale was finalized, the building was clean, plans had been drawn up and construction would begin the following Monday.

The men Remy and Hank had hired to staff this branch of the Brotherhood Protectors stood around him, ready to begin their new adventure.

"I bet none of you expected to be hauling off junk, cleaning and painting as a part of your duties working with the Brotherhood Protectors. But thank you for your hard work and patience. The contractor will take it from here and make this a place to be proud of."

"I don't know about all of you," Gerard said, "But I'm already proud of our new digs."

"Damn right," Lucas LeBlanc seconded. "Feels good to work with my hands."

"We'll be doing some of that when we get the boat manufacturing set up. It'll fill the gaps between assignments."

"I'm just glad to be back in Louisiana," Sinclaire Sevier said. "I've missed the heat and the humidity so thick you can slice it with a knife."

"Said no one ever," Rafael Romero said.

"Hasn't seemed to bother you, Romeo," Valentin Vachon said. "You've already been panting after the pretty gift shop owner. Too bad she wants nothing to do with you."

Romeo lifted his chin. "She's a work in progress. She'll come around eventually. What about you and the cute schoolteacher? I've seen you chatting her up every chance you get."

Valentin frowned. "Nothing going on there. I'm just being polite."

"Yeah, right." Landry Laurent shook his head. "Keep telling yourself that. Before you know it, you'll be married with two-point-five children in tow."

"Never happen," Valentin said and changed the subject. "Who's up for a beer?"

All ten men shouted a resounding, "Me!"

"Crawdad Hole in ten minutes?" Beaux Boyette said.

The men dispersed, heading for their vehicles.

Remy was the last man to leave the building, turning to lock it before climbing into his air-conditioned truck. He would go to the Crawdad Hole but only stay a few minutes, preferring to be at home with his fiancée. They'd picked a date over a year out from their engagement, only to move it up eight months because they'd been a little careless about contraceptives.

Remy grinned. Shelby was pregnant.

They couldn't be happier. As her sister had said more than once, they weren't getting any younger. If they wanted as many kids as Chrissy and Alan, they'd have to get moving. And the competition was getting tougher.

Chrissy was pregnant as well, with their sixth, due around the same time as Shelby and Remy's first.

Remy had come home. He had a big job ahead of him managing the Bayou Brotherhood. He had a good team and Hank Patterson behind him.

Now that they had the building cleared and the men had all either settled in the boarding house or other accommodations, it was time to take on the work they'd come to do.

Remy shifted into drive and started to leave the parking lot when a truck pulled in and came to a stop beside him.

A woman with sandy-blond hair and gray eyes lowered her window. "Are you Remy Montagne?"

He nodded. "I am."

"I'm Bernie Bellamy of Bellamy Acres."

"The farm just outside of town?"

"That's me," she said. "I'd heard you and Shelby were able to stop a cartel from using our town in their drug trafficking operations and how you had that man, Thomas Sanders, arrested for the murder of Ethan Fontenot."

"Yes, ma'am," Remy said. "That's all true."

After they'd subdued Sanders' henchman and Lissette, the sheriff had set up a sting with the DEA. Lissette had confessed to accessory to murder for a lighter sentence and spilled everything she knew about Thomas Sanders. The sting operation netted Sanders and a stockpile of crates full of drugs.

"I asked Shelby if she could help me," Bernie said. "She told me I should speak with you."

"About?" he prompted.

"She said you could help me with a problem I've had recently."

"What kind of problem?"

"Someone is sabotaging my business," Bernie said.

"The sheriff's department has no leads, and it's getting more personal."

"How so?"

She tipped her head toward the bed of her truck. "They killed Gertrude."

"Killed who?" Remy dropped down from his truck and strode to the back of hers.

Bernie got out and joined him.

In the truck bed was what appeared to be a large white, dead bird.

"Gertrude was one of the geese I use to keep the bugs down in my garden. I found her lying on my front porch; her neck was broken." She looked at her dead goose and then at Remy. "Can you help me?"

Not exactly what Remy had expected as their first assignment after protecting Shelby, but he knew they'd work it. Someone needed help. They were there to provide it.

"Miss Bellamy," he started.

"Ms. Bellamy," she corrected. "I'm a widow."

"Ms. Bellamy, we'd be glad to help you. I'll send someone over right away."

"I don't have much money to pay you with, but I can trade your services for my produce."

"We'll work it out," he assured her.

Bernie gave him a weak smile. "Thank you. I didn't know where else to go."

"You've come to the right place. The Bayou Brotherhood Protectors are here to help."

As Bernie climbed into her truck and left, Remy was already on his phone.

"Gerard, I have an assignment for you."

"Great. I'm ready. What do I have to do?"

"I need you to find out who killed Bernie Bellamy's goose."

"I'm sorry. Did you say goose?"

"I did." Remy grinned.

"Uh. Okay. I guess," Gerard said. "When do I start?"

"No time like the present."

"Gotcha."

Remy gave him the details and ended the call. As he climbed back into his truck and shifted into drive, he couldn't help thinking…

And so, it begins.

COLORADO COLD CASE

BROTHERHOOD PROTECTORS
COLORADO BOOK #8

New York Times & USA Today
Bestselling Author

ELLE JAMES

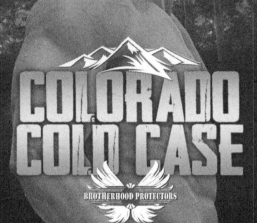

PROLOGUE

"What are we waiting on?" John "Griff" Griffin murmured as he held his position and waited for the go-ahead from the team lead.

"What's your hurry?" Freddy "Mercury" Rodriguez answered. "Got a hot date back in the States?"

"Maybe," Griff admitted. *If she hasn't already forgotten I exist*, he thought.

"That black-haired, green-eyed beauty you met at McP's?" Merc asked.

"Maybe," Griff repeated. He didn't like to own up to having a thing for anyone. Their lives belonged to the Navy. It was foolish to think he could maintain a relationship, much less start one, when they were at the beck and call of the military.

As highly trained Navy SEALs, their lives weren't their own. Not as long as they stayed in the military.

He'd met her the last time his team had visited their favorite bar, McP's, in San Diego. They'd been on three dates before his team had gotten called up for a mission. He hadn't even had time to let her know he'd be gone or for how long. They never knew.

The longer they were away, the less likely she'd be around when he returned.

Trouble was…he liked this one. A lot.

"Let's get this operation over with already," Griff muttered.

"Hey, Griff, what's it look like on point?" JJ Roberts's voice sounded in Griff's headset.

Griff studied their target, the building at the center of the little village in Syria. "Quiet. Nothing moving, not even the guard in front of the target building. I think he's asleep."

"I count two sentries on the main road leading into the village, leaning with their backs against a couple of homes," JJ said.

"Got two on the other end of town, same situation. Leaning with their AK-47s slung across their bodies," Derek Badger's gravelly voice hummed in Griff's ear.

Griff's gut tightened. "Too easy," Griff said softly.

Peter "Crack" Weissmuller chuckled. "Only easy day was yest—"

"Yeah. Yeah," Fridge, their team leader, said. "Focus on the objective."

They were there to extract a US citizen being held for ransom by ISIS – the Islamic State.

The Black Hawk helicopter had dropped them on the other side of a hill to avoid alerting ISIS to their imminent arrival. After a quick hike up and over the hill, they'd made their way to the village.

The team of eight Navy SEALs was tasked with extracting the citizen and getting him out of the country. Alive. If that meant taking out a handful of ISIS bastards, then so be it. Preferably with no civilian casualties, as always.

The ISIS abductors had purposefully chosen a quiet village full of civilians to surround them.

Wading through homes with women and children was like walking through a field of landmines. They had to make certain they didn't set any off and create collateral damage that would be reported on Al Jazeera the next day with images of the bloody bodies of children to remind the natives why they should hate the US.

"Ready when you are, Griff," Fridge said. "We've got your six."

Griff glanced across at his sidekick, Merc, and nodded. While Griff provided cover, his teammate gave him a thumbs-up and took off toward the target building, rushing forward and hugging the shadows of the mud and brick homes. When he reached a house one building short of their destination, he stopped and waited for Griff to leapfrog to the corner across from him.

Griff glanced behind him.

Fridge and Marty Sorenson brought up their rear. Crack and William "Willy" Daniels moved in from the opposite direction while JJ and Badger covered the town entrance.

Armed with a submachine gun and a nine-millimeter Glock, Griff took out his KA-Bar knife and slipped silently up to the guard at the front entrance to the building.

The man, dressed in the black clothing of the ISIS rebels, let the strap on his Soviet-made PKM machine gun do the work of holding the weapon in front of him. He was so sleepy that he didn't see Griff approach, nor did he have time to call out a warning to anyone inside or nearby.

Griff quietly dispatched the guard and dragged him into the shadows. He removed the bolt from the machine gun and slipped it into his pocket, rendering it ineffective. It would not be used against them that night.

He gave Merc a "follow me" sign. "Going in," he whispered into his headset.

"Right behind you," Merc said.

Griff pulled his night-vision goggles down over his eyes, pushed open the front door and entered, his machine gun with a silencer in place leading the way.

Merc followed.

Crack and Willy would bring up the rear, with Fridge and Marty covering the building from the outside.

One by one, they cleared each room, the soft sound of silenced gunfire barely making enough noise to rouse the ISIS soldiers from their sleep.

By the time they reached the locked door at the rear of the building, they'd dispatched nine ISIS rebels with no resistance.

The last door had a padlock on the outside of the door.

Griff slid his night-vision goggles up. Merc aimed the beam of his penlight at the lock while Griff pulled the bolt cutter from where it was strapped to his back and made quick work of the master lock on the hasp.

With the lock gone, the door swung open. Mercury shined his flashlight into the dark room.

The stench hit Griff first.

A man lay on the floor beaten, bloody, covered in excrement and so filthy Griff wasn't sure the man was Joe Franklin, the nephew of Senator George Franklin. Was this the American they'd been sent to rescue?

Griff bent over the man and rolled him onto his back. "What's your name?"

The man groaned something unintelligible.

"Boys," JJ's voice sounded in Griff's ear. "We've got

company. Looks like a whole company of ISIS headed our way in a convoy of trucks."

"Name!" Griff said more urgently.

The man forced sound through swollen lips. "Joe."

"Good enough," Merc said. "Get him out of here."

"Wrap it, Griff," Fridge said. "We have a date with a helo I don't plan to miss."

Griff bent, forcing back his gag reflex, grabbed the man's arm and pulled him up over his shoulder in a fireman's carry.

The hallways were too narrow for Merc to help. Griff had to carry the man out on his own. He'd been beaten so severely that he couldn't help himself, and it was like carrying a dead man. One who moaned every time his ribs bounced against Griff's armor plating.

"I hope you're on your way out of the village," JJ said. "They're coming in fast."

Gunfire sounded.

"Who opened fire?" Fridge demanded.

"None of us," JJ answered. "They're firing into the air. I won't be able to hold them off for long."

"Don't try," Fridge said. "Get back and head for our extraction point."

Griff emerged from the building, straining beneath the man's weight on his back.

Merc trotted along beside him. "Let me help."

"Help by getting us out of this shit hole before all hell breaks loose," Griff said through gritted teeth.

"Crack and Merc, take point. Marty and I will have your backs," Fridge said. "Go!"

Crack and Merc led the way through the small village, heading back the way they'd come—not by the road leading in from north to south. They headed west toward the hill, on the other side of which the Black Hawk waited for the signal to fly in and extract the team and their target.

The quiet village was now a cacophony of gunfire and shouts.

Where they had met little resistance coming in, now, people stumbled out of homes, armed and ready to fight.

If they held a gun, Merc and Crack took them out before they could fire on them first.

Griff ran with a lumbering gait, weighed down by the man draped over his shoulder. Somewhere between bumping into walls and bouncing against what Griff suspected were broken ribs, Joe had passed out.

Ahead, between two mud and stick structures, Griff caught a glimpse of the open field beyond and the Black Hawk rising above the ridge.

All he had to do was get his burden to the middle of that field and onto the chopper. His goal clear, and his focus lasered in on the helicopter, Griff pushed himself harder, picking up speed.

He burst out into the open, still running, careful not to stumble over brush or rocks. If he went down, he wasn't sure the man he carried could take the fall. Hell, he wasn't sure he'd be able to get back up himself, much less collect Joe and get moving again. He'd do his best to stay on his feet and keep his forward momentum.

Merc and Crack fell back and covered for him as he charged toward the Black Hawk swooping toward him into the field.

Gunfire erupted behind him.

Griff didn't look back. When he got Joe on board, he'd turn and help the others. Until then, he had one job, and he'd damn well better get it right.

As the Black Hawk hovered above the field, the gunner hanging out the side door opened fire with his fifty-caliber machine gun.

Fuck. That meant the guys behind Griff were in trouble.

Griff kept moving, closing the gap to where the chopper was descending.

Finally, the bird was down. Ten yards. Just ten yards.

His shoulder, back and legs screaming from the weight, Griff rushed forward. The medic inside the craft grabbed Joe as Griff flipped him off his shoulder. Together they lowered him to the metal floor of the chopper.

As soon as Joe was down, Griff spun, swung his machinegun around and ran back toward the others.

Merc and Crack were only steps away. All three

turned and covered for Willy, JJ, Badger, Marty and Fridge as they emerged from the shadows of the village.

Not far behind, men in black poured from between the huts like so many ants streaming from a hive.

With the help of the helicopter's gunner, Griff, Merc and Crack fired on the ISIS rebels, forcing them back to the cover of the buildings.

Willy, JJ and Badger raced past Griff and leaped onto the chopper.

Marty and Fridge were the last to approach.

Marty went down less than five yards from Griff.

Fridge scooped him up, flung him over his shoulder and kept coming.

As soon as they passed him, Griff shouted to Merc and Crack. "Go! I'll cover."

The men backed toward the helicopter, continuing to fire as they did.

"Griff, get in!" Fridge yelled into Griff's headset. "This bird's gotta fly."

Griff turned and ran for the chopper, already lifting off the ground.

He dove for the door.

Hands reached out for him. He grabbed hold of Fridge and Merc's hands. Together, they pulled him up as the chopper rose into the air.

Griff's legs dangled in the air for several heart-stopping moments while the gunner rained fire onto the ISIS rebels below.

Fridge and Merc dragged him onto the chopper. All three men collapsed onto the floor, breathing hard.

"We're not out of the woods yet," Badger's voice sounded in Griff's radio headset.

Griff sat up in time to see a truck spinning out into the field they'd just left. It stopped, and a man leaped out, placed an RPG across his shoulder and fired.

"Incoming!" Badger called out.

A second later, the Black Hawk shuddered violently. Where the gunner had been was a gaping hole. The engine sputtered and died. The rotors slowed, and the entire craft plummeted to the earth.

The last thing Griff heard was Crack yelling, "Fuck!"

ABOUT THE AUTHOR

ELLE JAMES also writing as MYLA JACKSON is a *New York Times* and *USA Today* Bestselling author of books including cowboys, intrigues and paranormal adventures that keep her readers on the edges of their seats. When she's not at her computer, she's traveling, snow skiing, boating, or riding her ATV, dreaming up new stories. Learn more about Elle James at www.ellejames.com

Website | Facebook | Twitter | GoodReads | Newsletter | BookBub | Amazon

Or visit her alter ego Myla Jackson at
mylajackson.com
Website | Facebook | Twitter | Newsletter

Follow Me!
www.ellejames.com
ellejamesauthor@gmail.com

ALSO BY ELLE JAMES

Shadow Assassin

Bayou Brotherhood Protectors

Remy (#1)

Gerard (#2)

Lucas (#3)

Beau (#4)

Rafael (#5)

Valentin (#6)

Landry (#7)

Simon (#8)

Maurice (#9)

Jacques (#10)

Delta Force Strong

Ivy's Delta (Delta Force 3 Crossover)

Breaking Silence (#1)

Breaking Rules (#2)

Breaking Away (#3)

Breaking Free (#4)

Breaking Hearts (#5)

Breaking Ties (#6)

Breaking Point (#7)

Breaking Dawn (#8)

Breaking Promises (#9)

Brotherhood Protectors Yellowstone

Saving Kyla (#1)

Saving Chelsea (#2)

Saving Amanda (#3)

Saving Liliana (#4)

Saving Breely (#5)

Saving Savvie (#6)

Saving Jenna (#7)

Brotherhood Protectors Colorado

SEAL Salvation (#1)

Rocky Mountain Rescue (#2)

Ranger Redemption (#3)

Tactical Takeover (#4)

Colorado Conspiracy (#5)

Rocky Mountain Madness (#6)

Free Fall (#7)

Colorado Cold Case (#8)

Fool's Folly (#9)

Colorado Free Rein (#10)

Rocky Mountain Venom (#11)

Brotherhood Protectors

Montana SEAL (#1)

Bride Protector SEAL (#2)

Montana D-Force (#3)

Cowboy D-Force (#4)

Montana Ranger (#5)

Montana Dog Soldier (#6)

Montana SEAL Daddy (#7)

Montana Ranger's Wedding Vow (#8)

Montana SEAL Undercover Daddy (#9)

Cape Cod SEAL Rescue (#10)

Montana SEAL Friendly Fire (#11)

Montana SEAL's Mail-Order Bride (#12)

SEAL Justice (#13)

Ranger Creed (#14)

Delta Force Rescue (#15)

Dog Days of Christmas (#16)

Montana Rescue (#17)

Montana Ranger Returns (#18)

Hot SEAL Salty Dog (SEALs in Paradise)

Hot SEAL,Hawaiian Nights (SEALs in Paradise)

Hot SEAL Bachelor Party (SEALs in Paradise)

Hot SEAL, Independence Day (SEALs in Paradise)

Brotherhood Protectors Boxed Set 1

Brotherhood Protectors Boxed Set 2
Brotherhood Protectors Boxed Set 3
Brotherhood Protectors Boxed Set 4
Brotherhood Protectors Boxed Set 5
Brotherhood Protectors Boxed Set 6

Iron Horse Legacy

Soldier's Duty (#1)
Ranger's Baby (#2)
Marine's Promise (#3)
SEAL's Vow (#4)
Warrior's Resolve (#5)
Drake (#6)
Grimm (#7)
Murdock (#8)
Utah (#9)
Judge (#10)

The Outriders

Homicide at Whiskey Gulch (#1)
Hideout at Whiskey Gulch (#2)
Held Hostage at Whiskey Gulch (#3)
Setup at Whiskey Gulch (#4)
Missing Witness at Whiskey Gulch (#5)
Cowboy Justice at Whiskey Gulch (#6)

Hellfire Series

Hellfire, Texas (#1)

Justice Burning (#2)

Smoldering Desire (#3)

Hellfire in High Heels (#4)

Playing With Fire (#5)

Up in Flames (#6)

Total Meltdown (#7)

Declan's Defenders

Marine Force Recon (#1)

Show of Force (#2)

Full Force (#3)

Driving Force (#4)

Tactical Force (#5)

Disruptive Force (#6)

Mission: Six

One Intrepid SEAL

Two Dauntless Hearts

Three Courageous Words

Four Relentless Days

Five Ways to Surrender

Six Minutes to Midnight

Hearts & Heroes Series

Wyatt's War (#1)

Mack's Witness (#2)

Ronin's Return (#3)

Sam's Surrender (#4)

Take No Prisoners Series

SEAL's Honor (#1)

SEAL'S Desire (#2)

SEAL's Embrace (#3)

SEAL's Obsession (#4)

SEAL's Proposal (#5)

SEAL's Seduction (#6)

SEAL'S Defiance (#7)

SEAL's Deception (#8)

SEAL's Deliverance (#9)

SEAL's Ultimate Challenge (#10)

Texas Billionaire Club

Tarzan & Janine (#1)

Something To Talk About (#2)

Who's Your Daddy (#3)

Love & War (#4)

Billionaire Online Dating Service

The Billionaire Husband Test (#1)

The Billionaire Cinderella Test (#2)

The Billionaire Bride Test (#3)

The Billionaire Daddy Test (#4)

The Billionaire Matchmaker Test (#5)

The Billionaire Glitch Date (#6)

The Billionaire Perfect Date (#7) coming soon

The Billionaire Replacement Date (#8) coming soon

The Billionaire Wedding Date (#9) coming soon

Ballistic Cowboy

Hot Combat (#1)

Hot Target (#2)

Hot Zone (#3)

Hot Velocity (#4)

Cajun Magic Mystery Series

Voodoo on the Bayou (#1)

Voodoo for Two (#2)

Deja Voodoo (#3)

Cajun Magic Mysteries Books 1-3

SEAL Of My Own

Navy SEAL Survival

Navy SEAL Captive

Navy SEAL To Die For

Navy SEAL Six Pack

Devil's Shroud Series

Deadly Reckoning (#1)

Deadly Engagement (#2)

Deadly Liaisons (#3)

Deadly Allure (#4)

Deadly Obsession (#5)

Deadly Fall (#6)

Covert Cowboys Inc Series

Triggered (#1)

Taking Aim (#2)

Bodyguard Under Fire (#3)

Cowboy Resurrected (#4)

Navy SEAL Justice (#5)

Navy SEAL Newlywed (#6)

High Country Hideout (#7)

Clandestine Christmas (#8)

Thunder Horse Series

Hostage to Thunder Horse (#1)

Thunder Horse Heritage (#2)

Thunder Horse Redemption (#3)

Christmas at Thunder Horse Ranch (#4)

Demon Series

Hot Demon Nights (#1)

Demon's Embrace (#2)

Tempting the Demon (#3)

Lords of the Underworld

Witch's Initiation (#1)

Witch's Seduction (#2)

The Witch's Desire (#3)

Possessing the Witch (#4)

Stealth Operations Specialists (SOS)

Nick of Time

Alaskan Fantasy

Boys Behaving Badly Anthologies

Rogues (#1)

Blue Collar (#2)

Pirates (#3)

Stranded (#4)

First Responder (#5)

Silver Soldier's (#6)

Blown Away

Warrior's Conquest

Enslaved by the Viking Short Story

Conquests

Smokin' Hot Firemen

Protecting the Colton Bride

Protecting the Colton Bride & Colton's Cowboy Code

Heir to Murder

Secret Service Rescue

High Octane Heroes

Haunted

Engaged with the Boss

Cowboy Brigade

Time Raiders: The Whisper

Bundle of Trouble

Killer Body

Operation XOXO

An Unexpected Clue

Baby Bling

Under Suspicion, With Child

Texas-Size Secrets

Cowboy Sanctuary

Lakota Baby

Dakota Meltdown

Beneath the Texas Moon

Made in the USA
Las Vegas, NV
16 September 2023